JUSTICE FOR EMILY

Susan Beth Pfeffer

JUSTICE FOR EMILY

A YEARLING BOOK

Published by
Bantam Doubleday Dell Books for Young Readers
a division of
Bantam Doubleday Dell Publishing Group, Inc.
1540 Broadway
New York, New York 10036

Visit us on the Web! www.bdd.com

Educators and librarians, visit the BDD Teacher's Resource Center at www.bdd.com/teachers

ISBN: 0-440-41249-8

Reprinted by arrangement with Delacorte Press

Printed in the United States of America

March 1998

OPM   10 9 8 7 6 5 4 3 2 1

JUSTICE FOR EMILY

One

"Poor child."

Emily Lathrop Hasbrouck ran into Bessie Webber's arms. "Oh, Aunt Bessie," she said. "It's been so horrible."

"I know it has, sweet child," Aunt Bessie said. "I just thank the Lord that Alice was able to find you."

"We had a little bit to eat," Miss Alice said. "But we're both very hungry. Is there any supper left, Mother?"

"Of course there is," Aunt Bessie said. "I hardly ate, myself, I was so sick with worry. There's plenty for all of us. Emily, why don't you freshen up while Alice and I set the table."

"I can do that," Emily said, eager to prove how helpful she could be.

"I know you can," Aunt Bessie said. "But tonight you don't have to. Just wash your hands and face. I don't know what you've been through, but you could stand a good cleaning."

Emily thought about the long walk she had been on and nodded. The Webbers had an indoor bathroom, a luxury she had not enjoyed while living with her late aunt Mabel. Emily used the bathroom and washed her hands and face carefully. Her clothes must be a mess, she realized. It was so kind of the Webbers even to let her eat supper with them. In all the world, they were the only people she knew who would be willing to do that.

Emily was afraid she'd start crying again. It felt as if that was all she had done in the past few days, cry and make a fool of herself. She was not yet twelve years old, and already she knew she had no future. She swallowed hard and then splashed some cold water on her face. When she was much younger and living with her aunt Mabel, Bridget, Aunt Mabel's maid, would tell Emily to wash her face with cold water whenever she caught Emily crying. Aunt Mabel didn't like it when Emily cried, because it showed she wasn't grateful.

"Supper's on the table," Aunt Bessie called. Emily smiled at the sound of Aunt Bessie's voice. Aunt Bessie wasn't her real aunt. The only aunt Emily had ever really had was Aunt Mabel, and she was really Emily's mother's aunt. Emily had no family of her own, not since Aunt Mabel had died, just a few weeks earlier. That was when Emily had been sent to the Austen Home for Orphaned Girls and all the trouble had truly begun.

"I'm coming," Emily answered, and told herself that whatever she did, no matter what Aunt Bessie and Miss Alice said, she was not to cry. It was true Miss Alice had said Emily could stay with them, but Aunt Bessie hadn't been there to give her consent. Emily was sure she'd been sent to clean up just to give Miss Alice and her mother a chance to discuss Emily's immediate future. She only hoped they'd let her spend the night with them. In the morning, Emily was sure, she could figure out another plan.

"Supper isn't fancy," Aunt Bessie explained. "We weren't home this weekend to cook. But there's some cold beef and vegetables and fresh bread and butter. That should fill us up nicely."

"Thank you," Emily said. She waited for Miss Alice and Aunt Bessie to serve themselves before she took any food. And then she took only a little. She'd eaten at the Webbers' house several times in the past and had always eaten heartily, but this was different. This time she didn't want to seem greedy or undesirable.

"Is that all you're eating?" Aunt Bessie asked. "You'll starve if you don't take more than that."

Emily helped herself to more bread and butter. "I'm not very hungry," she said. "Honest."

"I suspect Emily is more tired than hungry," Miss Alice said.

"Oh, no," Emily said. "I'm not tired. I can help with the dishes after supper. Honest."

Aunt Bessie looked hard at Emily. "I don't know what you've been through since I saw you last. But you don't have to earn your supper or a place to sleep. Not tonight and not in this household. Now, eat as much as you want and when you're ready to talk, I'm ready to listen."

Emily nodded. She tore into the bread and butter, then helped herself to more beef and vegetables.

"We have a spare room for you to sleep in," Miss Alice said to Emily. "It's clean and there's a bed in there. I'll get linens and a blanket after supper."

"Thank you," Emily said. "I won't stay any longer than you want me to. I promise. I know I'm young, but I'm a good worker. I can find a job somewhere. In a factory maybe, or as a servant. I don't want to cause you any trouble."

"We'll worry about all that later," Aunt Bessie said. "How are you feeling now?"

"Better," Emily replied. "Should I tell you what happened?"

"I think you'd better," Aunt Bessie said. "Alice and I go away for two days, and when we come back, we find the whole town in an uproar."

"It all started right after you left," Emily began. "Gracie, she was my friend from the orphanage, she and I were walking back to the Austen Home when Harriet Dale and Isabella Cosgrove and Florrie Sheldon saw us. They were so mean to us. I know they're from the best families, but they were horribly cruel to Gracie and

Mary Kate and me. Mary Kate was my other friend at Austen, only she ran away this morning." Emily was silent for a moment. "I ran away too," she said. "I hope Mary Kate has better luck than I did. She's going to be an actress."

"I'm sure Miss Browne will find her before then," Miss Alice said. Miss Browne was in charge of the Austen Home. She was a friend of Miss Alice's. Emily knew Miss Browne wanted to be nice to all the girls at the Austen Home, but she was beholden to the rich families in town for their charity to the orphans. Emily hoped for Mary Kate's sake that she became an actress real fast and never had to go back to the orphanage.

"Gracie and I were walking back and they saw us," Emily said. Of all the things she had to tell Aunt Bessie, this was the hardest. "They wouldn't let me walk on the sidewalk. They said I was an animal and I didn't deserve to, and whenever they'd see me walking on the sidewalk they'd push me down. So I stopped walking on the sidewalk and I'd walk in the street the way they told me to. It was easier than getting pushed all the time, and I couldn't fight back. Miss Browne said I couldn't."

Aunt Bessie put her hand out and took Emily's.

Emily took a deep breath. "Gracie didn't know I was walking in the street. And she got angry at Harriet and Florrie and Isabella for making us. That's when they said cruel things about Gracie. They used a terrible word, and that made Gracie even angrier. Gracie was the nicest girl, but she wouldn't let anyone say bad things about her parents. They were married, you know, and she was waiting for her mother to come back and get her. But they said bad things about her mother, and Gracie got really angry and she wouldn't walk in the street. So they pushed her."

"Who did?" Miss Alice asked.

"Harriet and Isabella," Emily said. "Florrie stood there and shouted for them to push Gracie. And when the two girls did, Florrie laughed. She laughed! Then Gracie fell on the street and she didn't get up. We saw that she'd hit her head on a rock. Harriet and Isabella ran. Only Florrie couldn't, because she's crippled. And then people came, but Florrie lied. She said it was all my fault it had happened, that Gracie and I had been teasing her and that we were running away and Gracie had tripped and hit her head. That wasn't what happened at all. They pushed her and Gracie died, but nobody would believe me when I said so."

"Did you tell Miss Browne?" Aunt Bessie asked.

"Of course I did," Emily said. "But she said it didn't matter. And they buried Gracie in the potter's field. Miss Browne felt bad about it, I know. She cried. But that didn't help Gracie any. And Mary Kate ran away because Gracie was the best friend she had. And I ran away too, to find my sister. You told me where she lived and I went to find her."

"I feel terrible about that," Aunt Bessie said. "I never should have told you."

"I'm glad you did," Emily said. "Please don't feel terrible. I never even knew I had a sister until my aunt Mabel died. It's only then that I found out about her. My mother died giving birth to her, and my father gave her to a couple to adopt. Once I knew I had a sister somewhere in the world, it made me feel better about things. I still felt lonely at Austen, though. It didn't seem to matter how many girls lived there with me. It's a terrible kind of lonely to have no family. It didn't even help that I had Gracie and Mary Kate to be my friends. But I could make up stories about my sister and how happy she was and how her family would love me and take me in once we found each other. Only they were just stories."

Emily thought back to that afternoon, to her excitement at the thought of meeting her very own sister. She swallowed hard to keep the tears from coming.

"I didn't get to meet her," she said. "I met her father, Mr. Smiley. He said I was never to meet her, never to try. He said he knew Judge Cosgrove and Judge Cosgrove had told him about Isabella and Gracie and me. Only Judge Cosgrove knew the lies, not what really happened. And Mr. Smiley believed the lies and he said if I ever tried to see his daughter, to see my sister, he'd have me put in jail. He threatened to do terrible things to my sister. He said he'd have to discipline her to see to it she didn't end up wicked, the way my father had been. The way I was. I couldn't let him hurt her. I don't even know her name, but she's my sister, and it would be terrible if she was hurt because of me. She doesn't even know I exist. How could I hurt her?"

"It's all right," Aunt Bessie said. "I'm sure Mr. Smiley said half those things just to frighten you away."

"I don't think so," Emily said. "Anyway, he drove me in his automobile and dropped me off and told me to walk back to Oakbridge if I wanted. He said he was sure Miss Browne and Judge Cosgrove had found someplace for me to go. Probably an orphanage in the city somewhere. Everyone says they're terrible places, but there's noplace else for me. Not unless I can find work somewhere. It doesn't matter. In a couple of years I'll be fourteen and then I can surely find a job. I can get by until then, I'm sure. But I am terribly grateful to you for putting me up for the night. I'm so tired, and you're so very kind."

"You're no trouble to be kind to," Aunt Bessie assured her. "And as long as you're under this roof, you'll never have to worry about being sent to one of those city orphanages. I can promise you that."

Emily nodded. She knew how kind Aunt Bessie was. Miss Alice was the town librarian and Aunt Bessie, her mother, was the telephone operator. They had befriended Emily, shared meals with her, and they'd even let her play their piano. The piano had been Emily's one true pleasure while she lived with Aunt Mabel. For the last year of Aunt Mabel's life, Emily hadn't even been able to go to school. Aunt Mabel had given her lessons at home instead, while Emily had cleaned and tended to her aunt. But Aunt Mabel had allowed Emily to have piano lessons and had even encouraged her to play. It had something to do with Emily being half Lathrop, Emily knew. The Lathrops were a respectable family, unlike the Hasbroucks, Emily's father's family. The Lathrops might fall on hard times, but they were always respectable, and respectable people did things like play the piano.

Emily almost laughed. What difference did it make that she was half Lathrop, half respectable? As far as the people of Oakbridge were concerned she was trash, plain and simple. A girl who would tease a poor cripple like Florrie Sheldon. A girl who didn't even have the decency to appreciate the charity that had been shown her. The Austen Home had bent its rules to let her in. Had Emily been thankful? Not for a moment. She had caused trouble. She had gotten into a fight with Harriet, Isabella, even Florrie. She'd never learned her place. The good people of Oakbridge wanted nothing to do with her. The good people, except for Aunt Bessie and Miss Alice, that is.

Emily looked straight at Miss Alice. Aunt Bessie was too softhearted to give her an honest answer. "Will you get in trouble because of me?" Emily asked. "My staying here?"

"No one would dare," Aunt Bessie said.

"They might, Mother," Miss Alice said. "But we'll deal with it if it happens. Tonight you're staying with us, Emily. We'll see what tomorrow brings."

"Thank you," Emily said. "Might I go to bed now? I am awfully tired."

"Of course," Aunt Bessie said. "You get a good night's sleep. You'll be surprised how much better things will seem in the morning."

Emily got up and walked over to Aunt Bessie, who enveloped her in a hug. Emily tried not to cry, but she couldn't prevent a tear or two from falling. Aunt Mabel had never hugged her. Emily's father had, but he'd died when she was eight, and now that she thought about it, she couldn't remember his embraces without an equally strong memory of the smell of alcohol.

"I love you," she whispered to Aunt Bessie, not even caring whether Aunt Bessie heard her. It was enough to say the words.

"I know, child," Aunt Bessie whispered back. "Now go to sleep, and try not to have any dreams."

Emily nodded. But she knew, asleep or awake, she'd have more than her share of nightmares.

Two

Emily woke up the next morning unsure of where she was. There was something unreal about it all. Then she remembered she was staying with the Webbers, and what seemed so strange was the quiet. At the Austen Home there was always noise. Even when Emily had slept in the isolation room, she could hear the noise a hundred girls made first thing in the morning. But this morning the only sounds she could hear were birds chirping and the grandfather clock chiming at the half hour.

Emily wondered what half hour it was, and got out of bed. She suspected it was early because Aunt Bessie and Miss Alice were not yet awake. She tiptoed out of the spare room and down the stairs.

The grandfather clock said it was 9:30. Emily couldn't believe it. She had never slept so late in her life.

She went to the kitchen, searching for some sign of the Webbers, and found a note addressed to her on the table.

11

Dear Emily,

*Mother and I agreed you needed your sleep, so we
didn't wake you. Mrs. Macdonald won't be in today, so you have the house to yourself. There's food
in the icebox. Help yourself to whatever you want
for breakfast and lunch. We'll see you when we get
home from work.*

Cordially,
Alice

*P.S. Mother says you should play the piano for as
long as you'd like.*

Emily couldn't believe it. A whole day to do whatever she wanted with. A day when she could do nothing
but stay in bed and read. Or play the piano. Or prove
how useful she could be by finding some job, ironing or
mending, and doing it all on her own. It was magical.

She began by making herself breakfast. Her first
thought was to have bacon and eggs, maybe even pan-
cakes. But then she decided she was there on the Webbers' charity and shouldn't take so much of their food.
Just some bread and butter would do.

Emily imagined Aunt Bessie coming back from work
and finding her ironing and mending without having
eaten much at all. But the funny thing was, Aunt Bessie
wouldn't have been pleased. Aunt Mabel would have
been, because gluttony was a deadly sin and it was better

to feed the soul than to feed the body. Aunt Bessie seemed to believe you should feed both of them amply.

Still, Emily couldn't make herself cook the bacon and eggs. She compromised on oatmeal and poured herself a big glass of milk to go with it. Even Aunt Mabel had approved of oatmeal and milk.

After breakfast Emily washed the dishes. She wished that the Webbers had left their dishes to be done, but they hadn't. In fact, Emily discovered that there didn't seem to be much of anything she could do. There was no pile of ironing, no mending basket filled to the brim. The furniture was dusted and polished. The floors didn't need waxing or the carpets beating. The silver, what there was of it, was free of tarnish. The windows glistened and the books were all in alphabetical order.

Emily sighed. Mrs. Macdonald, the Webbers' house-cleaner, did much too good a job. And she supposed the Webbers themselves were not messy people. But with everything in order, there was no housework to be done.

Emily walked to the piano. This had been her dream for so long, to have uninterrupted time just to play. She sat on the piano bench and began practicing her scales.

It felt wonderful to sit there, hearing the music, feeling the joy that playing the piano always gave her. There was sheet music to choose from, and Emily contented herself playing ballads and ragtime. Aunt Mabel had preferred hymns, and Emily's piano teacher had taught classical music. It was fun playing the popular music she'd never had a chance to before. Emily even read the words and sang along with some of the tunes. Perhaps the Webbers would let her play for them. It wasn't as good as ironing and mending for them, but it would have to do.

Emily heard the noon whistle blow from the mill. She was startled at how much time had passed. She stretched and wondered what she should do next. Lunch, she supposed. And then an afternoon of what? Reading would be nice.

But as Emily made herself a sandwich from the leftover beef and bread, she thought harder about what she should be doing. It had been wonderful to play the piano for two hours, but a day consisting of nothing but playing the piano and reading was positively sinful. The Sabbath was the only day intended for rest, and even on Sundays Emily had had chores to do, both at Aunt Mabel's and at the Austen Home.

There was nothing that needed to be done, Emily told herself as she glanced wistfully at all the books the Webbers owned. And if she did nothing for one day, how bad could that be? She'd done nothing those days when she'd been locked in the isolation room at the orphanage. She'd spent just that past weekend doing nothing.

Nothing except feeling terrible, she thought. Nothing except remembering how Gracie had died.

Suddenly Emily knew what had to be done. Miss

14

Alice had told her the day before that there was a policeman who believed her story. Perhaps she could find him at the police station and explain to him just how Gracie had died.

Emily felt better once the decision had been made. She'd returned to Oakbridge for a reason. That reason was justice for Gracie. Only Emily had told the truth about what had happened. Harriet and Isabella and Florrie had lied about Gracie's death. Emily vowed that Oakbridge would learn the truth.

She knew where the police station was from her walks to and from school. It felt strange to be walking to town without fear of Harriet and the others. They were all in school. Now that she thought about it, she wasn't an Austen girl anymore, and Harriet, Isabella, and Florrie would have no excuse to bully her. She was a town girl, just as much as they were, living with a family that was every bit as respectable. It was just like when she lived with Aunt Mabel. Not the same as having a mother and father, a home, and a sister of her own, but better than living off the charity of strangers.

I'm a town girl, Emily told herself as she marched into the police station. I belong here. I have every right to be here and I have an obligation to tell the truth. Even so, the sight of the policeman sitting at a desk frightened her.

"What can I do for you?" he asked. "Shouldn't you be in school?"

"I . . . I don't know," Emily said. She hadn't given school a thought all day.

"You don't know if you should be in school?" the policeman asked.

"Not today, I shouldn't be," Emily answered. "I'll go tomorrow, but not today. Today I have business here." It made her feel better to word it that way. *Business* had a grown-up sound to it.

"What sort of business might that be?" the policeman asked.

"There's a policeman I want to see," Emily said, wishing Miss Alice had told her his name. "He believes me. I want to talk to him."

"A policeman who believes you," the policeman said. "Don't the other policemen believe you?"

"I don't know," Emily said. "Maybe you're the one who does."

"Tell me what your story is and then I'll tell you if I believe you," he said.

Emily nodded. "My name is Emily Lathrop Hasbrouck," she said. She always included the *Lathrop* in her name, the way Aunt Mabel had taught her to. "I was with Gracie when she died. Gracie Dodge. I was there and I saw it all. Harriet Dale and Isabella Cosgrove pushed her into the street and she hit her head against a rock and died."

The policeman stared at her. "You're that Austen girl," he said. "The one making all those accusations."

"Yes, I am," Emily said. "Well, I'm not an Austen girl

anymore. But I do accuse Harriet and Isabella. Florrie Sheldon too, because she told them to do it. The three of them are responsible for Gracie dying. I know because I saw it all."

"You say one of our men believes your story," the policeman said.

Emily nodded. "He knows I'm telling the truth because of where Gracie died. In the street, that is. It was the opposite way from the Home. Florrie said we were running back to the Home, but if we were, Gracie wouldn't have been in the street. So Harriet and Isabella must have pushed her." She took a deep breath. "I know Harriet and Isabella didn't mean for Gracie to die. But she did die and they're responsible and the police should do something."

"And what should the police do?" the policeman asked.

"I don't know," Emily said. "Arrest them, I guess."

The policeman laughed. "You think we should go to Mayor Dale's house and Judge Cosgrove's house and arrest their daughters? Should we go to Mr. Sheldon's house and arrest his daughter while we're at it?"

"Yes," Emily said. "And I don't see why you're laughing. *They killed Gracie.*"

"No, they didn't," the policeman said.

"But they did," Emily insisted. "I saw them. I'm telling you exactly what happened."

"All three girls tell the same story," the policeman said. "About how you and the Dodge girl were picking on Florrie Sheldon, her being a poor cripple, and how frightened they were of you. Austen girls have a reputation in this town for being kind of wild, especially a new one like you. Harriet and Isabella ran for help, which poor little Florrie couldn't do, and you and the Dodge girl were scared of what would happen to you when a grown-up saw what you were doing to that poor child. So you ran away. Maybe you were going back to the Home, or maybe you were running in the opposite direction. Florrie couldn't know where you were running to, just that you were running. The Dodge girl tripped over her own two feet, she was so scared of the trouble she was about to get into, and had the misfortune to strike her head on a rock. A terrible thing for poor Florrie to have to see."

"It was a terrible thing for me to have to see too!" Emily interjected.

"But you were responsible," the policeman said. "I'm not saying the Dodge girl deserved to die for what she was doing, although there are those in town who think she got her just deserts. But there's nobody who thinks that Harriet Dale and Isabella Cosgrove were responsible for any of it, and to accuse poor Florrie Sheldon that way is a positive sin."

"I'm not sinning," Emily said. "I'm not the sinner here. Harriet and Isabella and Florrie are. They're mean and they're cruel and they killed Gracie."

The policeman looked straight into Emily's eyes. "Let me give you some advice," he said. "There's nobody in this town who believes your wild accusations and there's nobody in this town who ever will. In fact, nobody in this town wants you here. So pack your bags and find someplace else to live before you hurt any more of the good folk of Oakbridge."

"But I haven't hurt any of the good folk of Oakbridge," Emily said. "It's the good folk of Oakbridge who've been hurting me."

"All the more reason, then, for you to leave," the policeman said. "Girls run away from Austen all the time. Two did just yesterday, I heard tell. You join them. Find your own kind and don't bother us."

"I was one of those two girls," Emily said. "And I'm back. I know one of the policemen in this town believes me. I want to talk to him."

"Maybe someone was foolish enough to believe you at first," the policeman said. "But whoever it was has learned different. The mayor's daughter wouldn't lie. The judge's daughter wouldn't lie. And the mill owner's daughter wouldn't lie. God-fearing, respectable people like that don't lie."

"And Austen girls do?" Emily asked.

"We share our town with you," the policeman said. "We let you go to school with our children. We attend church with you and we give you our charity. That's our Christian duty. But we don't have to be blind to the kinds of girls who end up there. Daughters of no-accounts, drunkards, and whores. The outcasts of society. It comes as no surprise to any of us when one of

19

you turns out bad. And there will never be a day in Oakbridge when the word of an Austen girl is taken over the word of a Dale or a Cosgrove or a Sheldon."

"But I'm the one telling the truth!" Emily cried. "They pushed her. They killed her."

The policeman shook his head. "Do us all a favor and leave town," he said. "Go to some other orphanage. Or find yourself a job somewhere. You're not too young to work. Just leave us be. Because the longer you stay in Oakbridge, the more trouble you're going to cause, and take my word for it, you're going to be the one who'll end up paying for it. Not a Dale or a Cosgrove or a Sheldon. Not in this town. So leave while you still have the chance, before the Dales and the Cosgroves and the Sheldons find out you're back."

"No," Emily said. "They're not going to chase me out of this town. I won't let them."

"You won't have a choice," the policeman replied. "But if you're fool enough to stay here, there's nothing more I can do except tell you to lie low, keep quiet, and remember your place. Now, you get out of here. I have work to do, to protect the decent people in this town."

Three

Aunt Bessie and Miss Alice arrived home at about the same time that evening. That surprised Emily because Aunt Bessie finished work at four and Miss Alice at five. But Aunt Bessie's arms were filled with packages. Emily figured she had gone shopping on her way home.

"There'll be plenty of wagging tongues tonight," Aunt Bessie said as Emily ran to help her unload the bags. "It was bad enough Janet Shaw was my saleslady. You know what a gossip her mother is. Irene Maddox and Agnes Dumont were in the emporium at the same time."

"We knew people would start talking sooner or later," Miss Alice said. "Now it will just be sooner."

"I suppose they would have known by tomorrow anyway," Aunt Bessie said.

Emily yearned to ask what the town would be talking about, but thought better of it.

"I don't know where to begin," Aunt Bessie said. "Alice, what time did Miss Browne say she'd be here?"

"Miss Browne is coming?" Emily asked.

"At seven," Miss Alice replied.

"Why is she coming here?" Emily asked. "I don't ever want to see her again."

"Seven," Aunt Bessie said. "Then let's just have a cold supper. It'll be easier."

"Why is Miss Browne coming?" Emily asked again. "Are you sending me back to Austen?"

"Child, even if we wanted to, they wouldn't have you," Aunt Bessie said. "Now, open these bags and tell me what you think. It's been a long time since I shopped for a girl your age."

"These things are for me?" Emily asked. "Why? I don't need anything."

"Emily, you came here with just the dress on your back," Miss Alice said. "And that dress doesn't even belong to you. It's an Austen uniform. You must have something to wear."

"I had to guess at your size," Aunt Bessie said. "But if it's a little big, you can always grow into it."

"Try on everything," Miss Alice said. "That way we can return your clothes to Miss Browne when she gets here."

Emily took the bags and went to the spare room. She couldn't remember the last time she'd been given new clothes. In spite of the dread she felt thinking about Miss Browne, she was eager to see what Aunt Bessie had bought.

She wasn't disappointed. There were two dresses in

the bag, a blue-and-white middy and a brown plaid. There were also undergarments, handkerchiefs, socks, shoes, and a nightdress.

"How are you doing?" Aunt Bessie called from downstairs.

"They're beautiful," Emily said. "Thank you so much." But then it occurred to her that perhaps the Webbers expected her to pay for the clothing. Why should they spend so much money on her? It was enough that they were giving her food and shelter.

It wasn't quite so much fun to try on the dresses when Emily regarded them as a debt she had no idea how to pay. She only hoped Aunt Bessie had found bargains.

Emily took off all the orphanage clothes and changed into the new ones. She picked the brown plaid dress to wear downstairs.

"My, you look pretty," Aunt Bessie said. "And every day your hair is getting longer. Soon we'll be buying hair ribbons for you."

Emily touched her head self-consciously. When she'd entered Austen all her hair had been cut off. It was growing back, but she still had a long way to go before she was ready for hair ribbons. "What do I owe you?" she asked. "For the clothes."

"You don't owe us anything," Aunt Bessie said. "They're gifts."

"Think of them as Christmas presents," Miss Alice said. "Christmas will be here before we know it."

Christmas was almost four months away. Did that mean the Webbers intended that Emily stay with them for at least that long? And if they were giving her clothes, then they certainly weren't planning on sending her to some other orphanage, or sending her packing to fend for herself. Emily felt a surge of happiness that nearly overwhelmed her. Four months, at least four months, with the kindest people she'd ever known.

Then Emily remembered that her birthday was in December. Maybe the Webbers were just waiting for her to turn twelve. Then they might start looking for a place where she could work.

Emily told herself not to worry. Four months was four months. She had no right to expect anything, and she knew the proper response to the Webbers' generosity was humble gratitude.

"Thank you," she said. "You're both so kind. I don't deserve anything this fine."

"That's her Aunt Mabel voice," Miss Alice said. "It gives me the willies every time I hear it."

"Don't tease the child," Aunt Bessie said. "It was our pleasure to buy you the clothes, Emily. Alice won't let me shop for her anymore, and I have so little need. I enjoyed my little trip to the emporium."

"Supper's ready," Miss Alice said. "Nothing fancy, I'm afraid."

Emily didn't care what supper was. She ate ravenously, even though she'd had a perfectly fine breakfast and lunch. After the meal, she washed and dried the dishes, relieved that the Webbers agreed to let her do that one task.

Miss Browne arrived promptly at seven. Emily tried not to feel afraid when she saw her. Miss Browne had never been mean to Emily. Even though Emily felt half her stay at Austen had been spent in the isolation room, she knew that punishments at other orphanages were much harsher.

"What a pretty dress," Miss Browne said. "I wish the girls at the Home could all have clothes as nice as that."

Emily knew that the girls were all clothed with material donated by Florrie Sheldon's father. That was one reason why it had been so important for Emily to put up with whatever bullying Florrie and her friends dished out.

"Thank you," Emily said. "Aunt Bessie bought it for me today at the emporium."

"We have Emily's old clothes in this bag," Miss Alice said. "For you to take back to the Home."

"Good," Miss Browne said. "I'm sure we'll be able to use them." She pursed her lips. "I don't know how much longer we can count on Mr. Sheldon's donations. He telephoned me today again to complain."

"What was it this time?" Miss Alice asked. In spite of Miss Alice's and Miss Browne's friendship, it still felt strange to Emily to be sitting in the Webber parlor, socializing with the woman who recently had such control over her life.

Miss Browne hesitated. "It seems he received a phone

call from the police today," she said. "The officer said that Emily had gone there to tell her story about Gracie's death. Mr. Sheldon let me know in no uncertain terms that he would not put up with any more attacks on poor Florrie. I told him I had no control over Emily, she was no longer an Austen girl, but he wouldn't listen. Once an Austen girl, always an Austen girl, I suppose."

"Emily, did you do that?" Miss Alice asked. "Did you go to the police station?"

"You told me there was an officer who believed me," Emily said. "I wanted to talk to him. I didn't know his name. But I spoke to someone else, and he said nobody believed me."

Miss Alice sighed. "I wish you hadn't done that without asking my permission," she said. "As it happens, I telephoned the police station myself this morning and spoke to the policeman who had seemed so friendly the other day. He said he no longer doubted Florrie's version."

"The Sheldons must have put pressure on him," Aunt Bessie said.

"Someone undoubtedly did," Miss Alice replied. "But Emily, you didn't help matters any by trying to speak with him."

"Won't anybody listen to me?" Emily asked. "What about the newspaper? You mentioned them also, Miss Alice."

Miss Alice shook her head. "I telephoned there as

well. I was told quite firmly that they were now more than satisfied with the police accounting."

"They're scared too," Aunt Bessie said.

"Who can blame them?" Miss Browne asked. "When a girl from an orphan asylum takes on the daughters of the mayor and the judge and the mill owner, it's hard not to be scared. I know I am."

"I'm not," Aunt Bessie said.

"Well, you have less to lose," Miss Browne said. "Emily, one reason I've come here tonight is to appeal to you. I know Gracie's death was a great tragedy in your life. It was in mine as well. But the Austen Home is dependent on the charity of men like Mr. Sheldon. If we lose his cloth, the girls will have to get their clothes from church poorboxes. And Mayor Dale and Judge Cosgrove are both on the board of trustees of Austen. If they feel you are typical of the girls there, they'll find ways of punishing all the others."

"How could they do that?" Emily asked.

"Many ways," Miss Browne explained. "All of them perfectly acceptable. They could make fourteen or even twelve the age at which girls would have to leave Austen. They could reduce the amount of money allotted us for food and heat. They could cut the number of staff members. The board has already been threatening to eliminate the post of nurse. They could close the west wing and force us to double the population in each dormitory. Shall I continue? Every item I've mentioned

27

has been discussed by the board at least once. Give them the excuse and they'd vote to do one or all of them."

Emily was silent. She had hated living at the Home, but she knew her time there had been short and not typical. The majority of the girls who lived there seemed content enough. They had food to eat and clothes to wear and beds of their own. It wasn't much, not compared to what the Webbers were sharing with her, but it was as good as a poor girl with no parents, no family, could hope for.

But Emily also knew she wasn't ready to let Harriet, Isabella, and Florrie get away with Gracie's death. "Has anyone found Mary Kate yet?" she asked instead.

"Not yet," Miss Browne said. "I worry so about that girl. She's only twelve. I hate the thought of her on the streets somewhere."

"I'm sure she'll be all right," Emily said. "She's going to be an actress. She's probably looking for a theater to work at."

Miss Browne sighed. "I pray that you're right. I pray for all our girls."

"Prayers are all well and good," Aunt Bessie said. "But in the meantime, what are we to do?"

Emily grew scared again. Two new dresses might not mean security after all.

"I spoke to Miss Upshaw today," Miss Alice said.

Miss Upshaw was the principal at Oakbridge Primary School. She hated Emily and had been the cause of much of Emily's unhappiness.

"What did she say?" Aunt Bessie asked.

"I didn't give her much of a chance to say anything," Miss Alice replied. "I told her Emily was staying with us for the time being and would be returning to school tomorrow."

"Tomorrow?" Emily asked.

"You can't hide in this house forever," Miss Alice said. "Not that it sounds as if you spent today hiding, anyway. You must go back to school."

"But that's where they all go," Emily said.

"Miss Upshaw pointed that out to me," Miss Alice said. "And I agreed it is an unfortunate situation, but there's no other choice. I really don't know how she'll handle it when Emily returns tomorrow, but I'm sure something will be worked out."

"I can't do it," Emily said, her voice full of emotion. "I can't go there tomorrow. I can't face them. Not yet. Please don't make me."

"The longer you wait, the worse it will be," Aunt Bessie said. "Emily, you know you didn't do anything wrong."

"That doesn't matter," Emily cried. "They pushed me and made me walk in the street and called me horrible names. They killed Gracie, and she never did anything mean in her life."

Miss Alice reached out to Emily and took her hand. "They won't hurt you," she promised. "They may call you names, but they won't hurt you. They're scared too. Remember, they know what they did. They know it was wrong even if they are hiding the truth from others. They don't want any more of a fuss than you do."

Emily shuddered, remembering Florrie Sheldon's face as she screamed for Harriet and Isabella to push Gracie onto the street.

"I will walk you to school tomorrow," Aunt Bessie said encouragingly. "You can go from school directly to the library. You liked working there."

"Can I work there again?" Emily asked.

"I've been hoping you would," Miss Alice said. "You're a wonderful assistant. I was thinking the money that you earn there might pay for piano lessons."

"Really?" Emily asked. "Is there someone I could take lessons from?"

"Of course there is," Aunt Bessie replied. "Mary Louise Bell teaches piano. She's a dear friend of mine. Perhaps if I ask her she'll let you have lessons at a reduced cost."

"I could do some housework for her," Emily suggested. "Tell her that, please."

"See, Emily," Aunt Bessie said. "See how much you have to look forward to. Working at the library and piano lessons. Your stay here won't be so bad."

"There's something else," Miss Browne said. "Emily, I've begun to search for your family."

"What family?" Emily asked. Surely Miss Browne knew about Emily's meeting with her sister's adoptive father. Miss Alice must have told her. But Emily knew she didn't have any other family for Miss Browne to find.

"Your Hasbrouck family," Miss Browne said. "I know you pride yourself on being a Lathrop, Emily. But that doesn't mean the Hasbroucks are any less your kin."

"But the Hasbroucks are no-accounts," Emily said. "Aunt Mabel said they were derelicts and sinners. Each and every one of them."

"Your aunt might have been wrong," Miss Browne said. "Your father wasn't a derelict, now, was he, Emily?"

In Aunt Mabel's eyes he certainly had been. "Is that what you're going to do with me?" Emily asked. "Are you going to send me away to live with Hasbroucks?"

"First we have to find them," Miss Browne said. "And of course if they're bad people, you won't have to live with them."

"You have to understand, Emily," Miss Alice said in a gentle voice. "Tim and I will be married this spring. I'll be going to live with him. I don't know where that will be yet. It depends on which hospital gives him employment."

"Can't I stay with Aunt Bessie?" Emily found herself asking. "Please. I'll do anything."

"Child, we're not going to put you out," Aunt Bessie answered. "You won't be roaming the streets. But if you do have family, that's where you belong. We owe it to you to find out if you do. You know how important kin are. Wouldn't you like to live with your aunts and uncles? You might have cousins your own age to play with."

"That would be nice," Emily said dully. She knew about aunts. She'd lived with one long enough. And she knew about strangers too. They might seem nice. They might even give you clothes and call it Christmas presents. But you couldn't count on them. Not really. You'd only be disappointed. You couldn't count on anybody if you were an orphan. Mary Kate had been right to run away. Emily could only wonder how long it would be before she too was fighting to survive on the streets.

Four

Emily held on tight to Aunt Bessie's hand as they approached the school. Emily's heart was pounding so fast and the terror inside her was so sharp, she had trouble breathing.

"It will be all right," Aunt Bessie told her. "Nobody's going to hurt you."

Emily liked Aunt Bessie. And she trusted her most of the time. But this day Emily knew horrible things were going to happen and nobody would protect her.

She reminded herself that nobody had protected her in the past either. She'd dealt with Harriet and the others by giving in to them. She supposed she could do something like that even now if she had to. It was all temporary anyway, until some horrible Hasbrouck took her and turned her into a beggar or a thief or something worse, just the way Aunt Mabel had always said they would. She wouldn't feel the pride of a Lathrop anymore.

Emily realized then that Harriet, Isabella, and Florrie

came from the best families in Oakbridge but that they were killers. How much pride would their families have? Maybe they were part Hasbrouck too. In spite of her fear, she smiled.

"That's the spirit," Aunt Bessie said. "You can handle whatever comes your way just as long as you can smile."

Emily's smile vanished instantly. "Don't make me go in," she begged. "I can study at home. Your home, I mean. Aunt Mabel used to teach me. I can teach myself."

"Nonsense," Aunt Bessie said. "Look what happened yesterday. We told you to stay in and relax, play the piano, have a pleasant, do-nothing sort of day, and you hied yourself over to the police station and stirred up a hornet's nest. You're too young to be left on your own, and Alice and I both work. You must go to school. Besides, you like learning. You like your teachers. I've heard you tell Alice that. And you have friends in school. The other girls from Austen. They're your friends, now, aren't they?"

"I guess so," Emily said. They certainly weren't her enemies.

"And with your pretty new dress, I'll bet you'll make lots of friends with the other town children," Aunt Bessie said. "All you'll have to do is avoid those three girls. I'm sure they'll be just as happy to avoid you."

Emily wished it would be that simple, but she knew somehow that it wouldn't be. "I'd rather be in a hornet's nest," she muttered.

Aunt Bessie stopped in her tracks and pulled Emily alongside her. "Now, listen to me, young lady. Nothing in this life is easy. If the Good Lord wanted things to be easy, He would have made every day Sunday. I didn't want my husband to die and leave me penniless with a child to raise. But that's what happened, and I learned a trade and raised a daughter I can be proud of. There was many a night I wept myself to sleep and woke up in the morning worrying about the mortgage. But I did it because I had to. You must go to school. You must face those girls. If not for your sake, then for your friend Gracie's. So stop feeling so sorry for yourself and get ready to stand up for who you are. Fight the good fight, child. Show the world just what you're made of."

"Yes, ma'am," Emily said.

"Very good," Aunt Bessie said.

Emily could feel the eyes of every student on her as she and Aunt Bessie crossed the schoolyard and walked toward the front door. As they got closer, Emily could see Miss Upshaw standing with her arms folded, blocking the entrance.

"Mrs. Webber," Miss Upshaw said. "I suggest you take that girl back home with you. She isn't welcome here."

"She's living in Oakbridge," Aunt Bessie replied. "This school is open to *all* the children of Oakbridge. You might as well acknowledge that and let her in."

"I will have her suspended," Miss Upshaw said. "Preliminary to her expulsion."

"You have no grounds," Aunt Bessie said. "Even if you believe Florrie Sheldon's story, the worst Emily did was tease her. The day children are expelled from school for teasing will be the day you have no children in this school. Let us in. Emily has a long day ahead of her and you're not helping matters any."

"And where are her schoolbooks?" Miss Upshaw asked.

For the first time, Emily became aware that all she was carrying was her lunchbag. All the other children, most of whom were watching them, had arms laden with books.

"I . . . I lost them," Emily said.

"You lost all your schoolbooks?" Miss Upshaw asked. "And how did you manage that?"

Emily knew exactly how. She had left them on the side of the road when she had run away on Monday, convinced she would never return to Oakbridge and would never need them again. "I don't know," she said. "I just don't have them anymore."

"I shall have to suspend you until you find those books," Miss Upshaw said. "School property is not to be lost so easily."

"She might never find them," Aunt Bessie said. "Are you going to suspend her for the rest of her life over some used textbooks?"

"Until proper restitution is made," Miss Upshaw said.

Aunt Bessie opened her purse. "Here's ten dollars,"

she said. "I'm sure that will cover the cost of the books. Now will you let the child in?"

The money clearly flustered Miss Upshaw. She held on to the ten-dollar bill as though she had never seen one before. "This is outrageous," she said. "You cannot buy this girl's entrance into my school."

"Then you shouldn't have set a price for it," Aunt Bessie retorted, beginning to lose patience. "You requested compensation, and here it is. Now, Emily, go in, child, and have a good day. I'm sure this is as bad as it will get." She bent over and gave Emily a kiss on her cheek.

"Thank you," Emily said. She had no idea how she could ever pay Aunt Bessie back ten whole dollars. Perhaps that would be next year's Christmas present.

"Scoot now," Aunt Bessie whispered, and Emily did. She ran past Miss Upshaw and found herself followed by a rush of other children.

It felt terribly strange to be in the school building again, and Emily realized that much of that feeling was because neither Mary Kate nor Gracie was with her. The three of them hadn't walked to school together after the first week, but they had always been together once the school day began. Now Emily was going to have to walk into her classroom alone. She lingered in the hallway until she spotted Miss Upshaw walking toward her room, and then she ran in to take her seat.

The Austen girls were seated in the back of the room.

They formed a block, since they all wore the same dull blue uniform. Emily took her usual seat, painfully aware of the gap left by the absence of Mary Kate and Gracie.

Emily's entrance was enough to make the other children whisper. Most of them turned around to see what was happening. When Isabella saw Emily, she screamed.

Florrie burst into tears at the sound. And Harriet stood up and pointed at Emily. "Get her out of here!" she cried. "I never want to see her again."

"Quiet, children," Mrs. Hearst, Emily's teacher, said. "All of you, I want quiet now!"

Harriet stopped talking. But Florrie continued to sob, and Isabella shrieked again.

Miss Upshaw stormed into the room. "The Hasbrouck girl is causing trouble again, I see," she declared. "Very well. I shall take her to my office and keep her there until I can see if suspension is in order."

"I don't think that's necessary," Mrs. Hearst said. "All Emily did was take her customary chair. It's hardly her fault if the other children reacted as they did."

"It's your job to maintain order in your classroom," Miss Upshaw replied.

"I'm aware of that," Mrs. Hearst said. "And I was in the process of restoring my class to its proper order when you came in. No doubt you misread the situation. But I'm sure I'll have things under control momentarily."

"I won't sit in the same classroom with her," Harriet said, pointing at Emily. "And you can't make me, either. I'll call my father and he'll tell you to suspend her."

"Mayor Dale will naturally be very upset when he learns that the Hasbrouck girl has returned here," Miss Upshaw said. "No doubt he'll feel better if he learns she's been in my office all day."

"But she can't stay in your office indefinitely," Mrs. Hearst said. "Emily is one of my best pupils, and I'm glad to have her back. I'm sure Harriet will adjust to her presence soon enough if we adults allow her to."

"Please don't let her near me," Florrie sobbed. "She wants to kill me. I know she does."

"Nobody will hurt you," Mrs. Hearst said. "I know we're still upset over Gracie's death. It was a great loss for all of us. And many of the children have reported having nightmares because of it. Seeing Emily back is a shock, although a happy one. We will be equally shocked and pleased when Mary Kate returns. Now, Miss Upshaw, why don't you return to your office? I know how much work you have to do, and we have an arithmetic lesson to get to."

"Emily has lost her schoolbooks," Miss Upshaw said.

"She can use Gracie's books," Mrs. Hearst replied. "Miss Browne was kind enough to return them to me."

"Please," Florrie sobbed. "Please don't make me sit in the same room with her."

Even Emily knew Florrie was sincere. She didn't feel sorry for her, but she could recognize the sound of genuine terror.

"Stand up, Emily," Miss Upshaw said. Emily did as she was told. "Take your desk and chair and put them in the hallway, outside the classroom door. You'll remain there until we decide what to do about you."

"I hardly think that is necessary," Mrs. Hearst said.

"I am the principal of this school," Miss Upshaw said. "And I am tired of people telling me what is necessary. Harriet, Isabella, and Florrie have endured a terrible shock and they must not be made to suffer anymore. Emily will be able to hear the lessons perfectly well from the hallway. She will get the education she is entitled to while disturbing none of the other children."

Mrs. Hearst sighed. "What about lunchtime?" she asked. "And recess? And art and music and gym?"

"She will remain in the hallway," Miss Upshaw said. "She will serve as an example to all the other Austen girls. An example that she should have set when she first entered this school, instead of being allowed to continue taunting the daughters of the good families of this town."

One of the Austen girls raised her hand. "It's not our fault Emily did all those bad things," she said. "She just came to live with us. We never liked her either."

"That's right," another Austen girl said. "She was kicked out of Austen because she wasn't any good."

"It is a shame she couldn't be kicked out, as you put it, from Oakbridge," Miss Upshaw said. "But there are some who have foolishly allowed her to remain with them. Nonetheless, as we all well know, the girls from

Austen must be carefully controlled, lest they become a bad influence on the others. And to see one of their own, even if that's no longer the case, treated as an outcast will serve as a reminder to them of how fragile charity can be, and how necessary it is to feel gratitude and humility at all times. In fact, perhaps it is better for Emily to remain at our school, in a state of permanent display, so to speak, than to have her expelled. For the bad behavior of one Austen girl reflects on all of them, and Emily's punishment, in its way, atones for all of them."

"Miss Upshaw, I hardly think Emily deserves unceasing humiliation," Mrs. Hearst said. "If you insist on her sitting in the hallway until the other children adjust to her return, then I can't argue with you. But to make her representative of all the Austen girls, when, as they have pointed out, she was hardly there for more than a month and no longer lives there, well, I just can't understand that."

"I have not asked for your understanding," Miss Upshaw said. "You have a soft spot for the Austen girls. That has been commented on by many of the parents and teachers. Perhaps too soft a spot. Perhaps if you had been more willing to discipline Emily, then Harriet, Isabella, and Florrie would not have had to suffer so. But that is history. What is important now is that the Austen girls, and I include Emily Hasbrouck in that group, understand the importance of humility and decent behavior. I expect every Austen girl in this school to write a two-page composition on the importance of accepting one's lot with Christian forbearance. Now, if you'll excuse me, I must go to all the other classrooms and inform the Austen girls of their new assignment. Good day, Mrs. Hearst. Emily, take that desk and chair and place them outside this door."

Florrie had stopped crying. Emily hoped she could keep herself from starting. As she lifted the desk to carry it outside, she turned to face the other Austen girls.

"We hate you," the girl nearest to her whispered.

Emily knew they did. She didn't blame them. She hated herself just as deeply for allowing Miss Upshaw to force her into the hallway. It was no different, she knew, than being forced off the sidewalk by Harriet and the others. Once again the good people of Oakbridge had pushed her into the gutter.

Five

The hardest part of sitting in the hallway wasn't loneliness, which Emily was accustomed to, or even the feeling that everybody hated her. The hardest part was concentrating. She couldn't always hear what Mrs. Hearst said, and she couldn't see the blackboard. It was easier to daydream than pay attention.

Emily knew all about the dangers of daydreaming. She had done nothing but daydream about the life she would have with her sister when she'd found her. It was going to be a glorious life, with a family that loved her. Only it hadn't come true. And her daydream that the Webbers would let her stay with them forever wasn't going to come true either. They'd soon realize she wasn't worth the bother, and she'd be made to live with some horrible Hasbroucks. Emily didn't care to daydream about that possibility.

The best she had to look forward to was some other orphanage taking her in. Emily had hated living at Austen, but from what she'd heard, it was the best of the lot. At the next home, she knew she'd never meet anyone like the Webbers, who invited her to eat with them and play their piano.

At least she wouldn't have Isabella screaming at the sight of her. And nobody would know her, so they wouldn't hate her. Emily remembered what it had been like when nobody hated her. She wouldn't mind going back to that, even if it meant wearing poorbox clothes, or begging on the streets.

Emily tried to hear everything Mrs. Hearst was saying. There seemed little point in getting an education, since she'd be on her own soon enough and the kinds of jobs she'd find would hardly require a knowledge of geography. But she liked school, and if this was all the schooling she was going to have, she might as well take advantage of it.

The bell rang for lunchtime. Emily could hear the children all getting up and preparing to leave their classrooms. She dreaded having them walk through the hall, seeing her and talking about her, but there was no way she could escape. She willed herself not to cry, to show she didn't care. She opened her geography book, Gracie's old book, and pretended to read about African tribes.

Even though she didn't look at the children as they walked by, Emily could hear their comments and laughter. Harriet kicked her in the leg, and it was all Emily could do to keep from crying out. But she didn't dare make a sound, for fear that Miss Upshaw would punish her.

To Emily's surprise, a girl came out of the classroom dragging a desk behind her. "Hello," she said. "I'm Constance Crawford. May I have lunch with you?"

Emily stared at her. She'd never had much of a chance to learn the names of the other children in her class. The Austen girls were supposed to keep to themselves, and there were so many of them, Emily had trouble keeping them straight.

"You shouldn't be here," Emily said. "You should be with the class."

"It's all right," Constance said. "I asked Mrs. Hearst if I could have lunch with you and she said yes. I have a liverwurst sandwich. What do you have?"

"Ham," Emily answered. "And an apple."

"I have an apple too," Constance said. "Would you like half of my liverwurst for half of your ham?"

"All right," Emily said. She handed over half her sandwich, almost expecting Constance to keep it and give her nothing in return. But Constance gave her half of her own sandwich.

"Why do you want to have lunch with me?" Emily asked. "The other children will hate you for it."

"They hate me anyway," Constance said. "I'm used to it. And I thought you might be lonely out here. I would be, even though everyone hates me."

"Why does everyone hate you?" Emily asked as she ate. "You're not an Austen girl."

"You don't have to be an Austen girl for everyone to hate you. Actually, most of the girls don't hate the Austen girls. They pick on them, but they don't hate them. I think they like having them around just so they can be mean to them. But it's hard to hate somebody who can't fight back."

"They hate me," Emily said.

"You must have fought back," Constance said. "Or done something different."

"I told them they had no right to be mean to me," Emily said.

"That would do it," Constance said. "They think they have the right. The rich children in this town are the worst I've ever seen."

"Have you seen a lot of rich children?" Emily asked.

"More than my share," Constance said. "My father is a lawyer who works for the union. The union is trying to organize the workers at the Sheldon mill here. This is my fourth school. Whenever the union tells my father he has to go where they're organizing, we all pack up and go with him. But this is the only town I've been in where there's a mill and an orphanage. Maybe that's why the rich children are so especially mean."

"I don't care why they're mean," Emily said. "I just wish they'd stop."

"You should always know why," Constance said. "That's what my father says. 'Know your enemy.'"

"I don't want to know my enemy," Emily replied. "And I wish my enemy had never gotten to know me."

Constance laughed. Much to Emily's surprise, she found herself laughing too.

"I like your hair," Constance said when they stopped laughing and resumed eating their lunches.

"You do?" Emily asked. "It's so short."

"Well, it looked awful when you first started school," Constance admitted. "But it's been growing out ever since. And I like short hair. It must be so much easier to take care of. And it reminds me of *Little Women*. You know the part when Jo cuts her hair? I always thought that was the bravest, noblest thing she could do. Have you read *Little Women*?"

Emily nodded. "When I lived with my aunt Mabel I read a lot," she said. "She let me play the piano, but that was the only noise she liked. So I had to read to keep quiet."

"It must be nice living in a quiet house," Constance said. "I have two older brothers, they're twins actually, and they make noise all the time. And my father is always having people over. Workers and union organizers and friends. He and my mother have lots of friends. My mother is a suffragette and lots of times she has meetings at our house."

"A real suffragette?" Emily asked. She knew Miss Webber thought women should be allowed to vote, but she didn't think that made her a real suffragette. "Has she ever been arrested?"

Constance nodded. "Lots. But never for very long. Sometimes she says she married my father because he's a lawyer and he can get her out of jail faster. Do you think women should have the right to vote?"

"I think I should," Emily said. "I'm not so sure about Harriet and Isabella."

Constance laughed. "My father hates Judge Cosgrove," she said. "Mayor Dale too. And he uses terrible language whenever he talks about Mr. Sheldon. Sometimes Mama threatens to wash his mouth out with soap."

"Would she really?" Emily asked.

"It's a joke," Constance replied. "They make jokes about each other. But he does use terrible language."

Emily remembered some of the names Florrie had called her. "He can call Mr. Sheldon whatever names he wants," she said. "I'd never wash his mouth out."

"He'll be pleased to hear that," Constance said. "Why don't you live with your aunt Mabel anymore?"

"She died," Emily said. "I lived with her for three years after my father died. My mother died when I was three, and then my father died when I was eight, and then my aunt Mabel died just last month."

"And then you went to live at Austen and then you disappeared and then you came back," Constance said.

"I didn't disappear," Emily said. "I just missed a few days of school."

"Everyone assumed you'd left town forever," Constance said. "That was all everyone talked about on Monday. How Gracie had died and you and Mary Kate had disappeared. Only she's still gone and you're back."

48

"The Webbers invited me to stay with them," Emily explained. "Do you know them? Miss Webber is the librarian and her mother is the telephone operator."

"I know the librarian," Constance said. "I go to the library whenever I can. I've seen you working there."

"I'm going to start working there again today," Emily said. "To earn enough money to take piano lessons."

"I wish I could play the piano," Constance said. "We don't own a lot of things because we have to move so often. And we never get settled in a town long enough to take lessons. My mother is a real lady. When she was a girl, she took dancing lessons and fencing lessons and all kinds of other lessons. But then she married my father and she never had the chance to dance or fence again."

"They sound very romantic," Emily said. "What are your brothers' names?"

"Tom and Ben," Constance said. "They're fourteen. When I was younger, sometimes the other children in my class would try to hit me, and they'd protect me. They protected each other when children tried to hit them. It's good having twins in the family."

"Why didn't the mill workers' children protect you?" Emily asked. "Didn't they know your father was trying to help them?"

"They were too scared to help," Constance replied. "They were afraid their fathers would lose their jobs if they had anything to do with a union organizer's daughter."

Emily looked at Constance. She had blue eyes, light brown hair, and a dusting of freckles. She was wearing a pretty yellow dress and had a big white bow in her hair. Emily would never have thought that this was a girl who had to worry about being hit or hated by other children.

"What's the matter?" Constance asked. "Do I have liverwurst on my nose?"

"No," Emily said. "I was just surprised, that's all. That you've had so many bad things happen to you."

"It hasn't been that bad," Constance said. "I think women should have the vote. And I think mill workers shouldn't have to work more than ten hours a day, and that they should have safe working conditions, and that children shouldn't be made to work either. Those are the things my parents fight for."

"But don't you wish the other children didn't hate you?" Emily asked. "Don't you want to have friends?"

"You could be my friend," Constance said. "Everyone hates you already and they hate me already, so we might as well. Would you mind being my friend?"

"I'd like it," Emily said. "But they'll take it out on you. I'm sure they will."

"I'll just have Tom and Ben beat them up," Constance replied. "Maybe you could come to my house for supper sometime. There's always someone having supper with us. It'd be fun if it was a friend of mine for a change."

"I'd like that," Emily said. She couldn't imagine having supper at a friend's house. She hadn't been invited to do that since Aunt Mabel had gotten sick.

"Oh, dear," Constance said. "They're coming back. I can hear them. I have to put my desk back in the classroom. I'll see you soon. And I'll have lunch with you again tomorrow. All right, Emily?"

"All right," Emily said. It seemed like a miracle that somebody actually liked her. For a moment she allowed herself the fantasy that all of Constance's family would like her, that they might invite her to stay with them. Even if they took her on as a domestic, Emily was sure they'd be kind to her. A domestic was a worker, after all, just the same as a millhand.

Emily laughed at herself. There she was, doing it again. She had met Constance only a few minutes ago, and already she pictured herself as part of Constance's family.

She buried herself in the geography book, taking care not to look at any of the children as they returned to the classroom. It was a comforting thought that Constance was in the room. It almost made it hurt less when Harriet kicked her again. Emily wasn't alone. There was someone who liked her, someone who wanted to be her friend.

She tried hard to listen to the lessons that afternoon, and when she felt the need, she stood up and peeked into the classroom to see the blackboard. Once she thought she heard Miss Upshaw walking down the hallway, and she raced back to the desk, lest she be found

51

standing up. But there was no Miss Upshaw, and soon she stood again. She felt more like a member of the class when she could see and hear all that was going on in the room. And she thought she saw Miss Hearst acknowledge her with a slight nod.

It isn't so bad, Emily told herself. And when the bell rang announcing the end of the day, it was an advantage to be in the hallway. Emily was the first one out of the school, so she didn't have to see Harriet and the others. She ran outside and went straight to the library.

"How was school today?" Miss Alice asked as Emily walked through the door.

Emily knew that Miss Alice didn't want to hear about Isabella screaming and Florrie crying. It would be bad enough when Miss Bessie told her that it had cost ten dollars to get Emily through the front door. And Miss Alice certainly wouldn't want to know that Emily had been forced to sit in the hallway. For that matter, Miss Alice and Aunt Bessie only wanted to hear that things were all right. They were performing an act of charity by allowing Emily to stay with them, and the one thing Emily knew from her years with Aunt Mabel was that charity cases shouldn't have any problems that had to be taken care of.

"School was fine," Emily said. "Once it got started. And at lunch today, I made a new friend. Her name is Constance."

Miss Alice rewarded Emily with a big smile. "I knew things would work out," she said. "A new friend on your first day back at school. I'm sure it's the start of a whole new life for you."

Emily nodded. She'd had more than her share of new lives in the past few weeks, but she was sure she could make it through another one, especially now that she had a real friend.

Six

Emily relaxed for a moment on Monday and allowed herself the luxury of thinking. Her class had just left for its music lesson. Emily, of course, remained at her desk in the hallway. It was still a struggle to hear everything that went on in the classroom, and she got nervous every time she stood to see the work on the blackboard. But most of the children had stopped laughing and making cruel comments about her as they walked through the hallway. Harriet still kicked her now and again, but even she had lessened her attacks. Emily knew Miss Alice and Aunt Bessie didn't need to know that her desk had been moved out of the classroom.

She smiled. Her life wasn't so bad at all. She had three meals a day, a roof over her head, and pretty new clothes, thanks to the Webbers. She was back working at the library, a job she enjoyed doing, and on Saturday, she'd been taken to Mary Louise Bell's house and had played the piano for her. Mrs. Bell had said she'd be delighted to give Emily piano lessons. So the money

Emily earned from her library work would go to pay for them, but as long as the Webbers took care of her, she didn't need money for anything else.

Constance had had lunch with her every day since Emily had returned to school. She'd even invited Emily over for dinner Thursday night. Emily had gotten the Webber's permission, and she was excited at the thought of going to a friend's house, just the way other girls did. Really, things weren't bad at all.

"Emily."

Emily looked up to see Mrs. Hearst standing beside her. "Yes, ma'am," she said.

"Miss Upshaw wants to see you in her office now," Mrs. Hearst said.

Emily's heart sank. "What have I done now?" she wondered aloud.

Mrs. Hearst shook her head. "I don't know," she said. "Maybe it's nothing. But Miss Upshaw told me to send you, and for you to bring all your things."

Emily got her books and walked down the hall to Miss Upshaw's office. How could she have done anything wrong? She had followed all Miss Upshaw's rules.

The school secretary told Emily to go into Miss Upshaw's office. Emily thanked her and walked in.

"Don't sit down," Miss Upshaw said. "I received a telephone call from Miss Browne. She wants you to go to the Austen Home immediately. There is no need for you to return to school afterward. That will be all."

Emily stared at Miss Upshaw. What did Miss Browne

want with her? She yearned to ask but didn't dare. "Thank you, ma'am," she said instead, and left the office.

The Austen Home was a short distance from the school. Emily was flooded with memories as she walked. Terrible memories of Harriet, Isabella, and Florrie tormenting her and her friends. And then the image of Gracie's last moments came back. It was a picture Emily tried hard not to think about. Her own life was going so well, and Gracie was dead. And what had Emily done to avenge that death? Nothing. She hadn't even learned the lesson Gracie had died for, that her rights were as strong as anyone else's. She'd accepted exile in the hallway, had said nothing when Harriet continued to abuse her, had been grateful that she'd been given as much as she had. Humble and grateful. Aunt Mabel would be proud indeed.

When Emily saw the Austen Home, she found herself almost unable to move. She had never been mistreated there, not really, but the institution represented loss and sorrow and little else to her. What did Miss Browne want? Had the Webbers decided she should return there? Had the asylum's trustees changed their minds and agreed she could return? Or had the Austen girls complained so bitterly to Miss Browne about Miss Upshaw's treatment of them that Emily had been sent to apologize and explain?

Emily forced herself to climb the steps and enter the

building. There were strict rules about the girls speaking and making noise, but even so the building seemed un- usually quiet with the girls still at school. Emily saw one of the matrons, who told her to go to Miss Browne's office.

Emily thought back to the first time she'd been in that office, her first day at Austen. She'd had hopes then. She'd had hopes the day she and Mary Kate had broken into Miss Browne's office and looked at Emily's papers to see what they could find about Emily's sister. But every other time Emily had been summoned to that office it was to be punished.

"Thank you for coming," Miss Browne said. "I thought if you came before the rest of the girls arrived, it might cut down on rumors and speculations. And Miss Upshaw was kind enough to let you leave school early."

"My class was at music," Emily said. "I'm not al- lowed to go there anyway."

"Yes," Miss Browne said. "Several of the girls have told me about Miss Upshaw's decision. I hope it isn't too hard on you."

"No," Emily said. "It's all right. Why did you want to see me?"

"Several reasons," Miss Browne said. "Sit down, Em- ily. First of all, I wanted to tell you somebody returned your schoolbooks to us. Your name was in them, and the person who found them learned you had been living here and brought them back. Have you been given other books to use in the meantime?"

"I'm using Gracie's books," Emily said.

"Why don't you bring these back to school tomorrow?" Miss Browne said. "They are school property, after all."

Emily thought about the ten dollars Aunt Bessie had paid for them and wasn't sure whom the books belonged to. But if that was the only reason she'd been summoned, she had nothing to complain about.

"Thank you, ma'am," she said. "May I go now?"

"No, there are other things as well," Miss Browne said. "You received this letter." She showed Emily the envelope. "If you were still an Austen girl, of course, we'd have read the letter before giving it to you. But since you aren't, I wanted to give it to you directly."

Emily took the letter from Miss Browne. "Thank you," she said. "I'll read it later."

"Would you do me the favor of reading it now?" Miss Browne asked. "I thought it might be from Mary Kate."

Emily examined the envelope. She could understand why Miss Browne had come to that conclusion. The handwriting was poor, just the way Mary Kate's had been. And besides, who else would be writing to Emily at the Austen Home?

She opened the letter, and it was from Mary Kate. Emily read it swiftly.

Deer Emily,

I have run away. I will never go back to Austen. I met a man and he says he will put me on the stage. He gives me food. And he says I have what men like.

I am leaving with him today. I dont know where we are going. He wont tell me. He says when we get there he will get me a job as an actress.

Do not run away. It is hard and you wont like it. I do things no proper girl should do. When I am an actress I will rite to you again.

Mary Kate

"Is it from Mary Kate?" Miss Browne asked.
Emily nodded.
"May I read it?" Miss Browne asked.
Emily handed the letter over. Miss Browne read it and gave it back to her.
"She's lost," Miss Browne said. "She's lost forever. That happens to so many of our girls, but few as young as she."
"You won't try to find her?" Emily asked.
"Even if we could find her, it would be wrong to bring her back," Miss Browne said. "We have good girls here. Mary Kate has been corrupted. Someday, perhaps, she'll go to a home for girls such as herself and find

redemption. But Austen is no longer the proper place for her."

Emily thought about Mary Kate. It had always been her desire to be an actress and to be kept by some rich man. Maybe the man she was with was rich. Maybe she would become an actress.

"It's what she wants," Emily said. "It's what she always wanted."

"It's what she always dreamed of," Miss Browne said. "But I don't think she understood the price she'd have to pay." She looked out the window for a moment. "But she is no longer our concern. I'll close the files on her when you leave."

Mary Kate had known that file by heart. Emily knew she wouldn't mind seeing it closed.

"Now let's talk about you for a moment," Miss Browne continued. "How are you enjoying your stay with the Webbers?"

"Just fine, ma'am," Emily said.

"They're very kind women," Miss Browne said. "I didn't grow up in Oakbridge, but I had family here, and I spent many summers visiting. I've known Alice Webber most of her life. She's always had a fondness for strays. You know, stray dogs and cats. She used to bring them back to Bessie and beg to let them stay. Bessie is softhearted herself and agreed more often than not. I think she'd still be doing it, except that dogs and cats make Tim sneeze something fierce."

Emily knew she was being compared to a stray dog

and didn't care for it. But she also knew there was an element of truth in the remark. Aunt Mabel's friends had called her a stray often enough.

"I expect I'll hear something about your Hasbrouck relatives soon," Miss Browne said. "And when they find out about your orphaned condition, I'm sure one of them will invite you to stay with them."

Emily scowled.

"If your aunt hadn't been so prejudiced against them, you would have been sent to live with them after her death," Miss Browne said. "Which would have been the best for everyone. The Austen Home never takes in girls over the age of twelve."

"I'm not twelve yet," Emily said.

"I know that," Miss Browne said. "You're three months short of it, and because of connections you were allowed to join us. But it didn't work out, as you well know. Your presence here was a terrible disruption."

"I don't live here anymore," Emily said.

"That's true," Miss Browne said. "But things aren't that much better for us with you staying with the Webbers. Our girls are being given additional assignments because of you. Miss Upshaw is monitoring them even more strictly than usual. And more than one member of our board of trustees has expressed displeasure that you've been allowed back into the community."

"What do you want me to do?" Emily asked. "Run away? Be like Mary Kate?"

"No, of course not," Miss Browne said. "I wouldn't

61

wish that for any girl. But when I do find some family member who is willing to take you in, you'll simply have to go with him. It's for your own good as well as the good of Austen. And it's wrong of you to take advantage of Bessie's and Alice's kind hearts."

"You haven't found my family yet," Emily said. "And you might not ever. They could all be in jail. Or they could be drunkards and wastrels."

"I hope for your sake that they aren't," Miss Browne said. "But even if they are, if one of them is willing to let you live with him, you must go. The Austen Home remains your legal guardian, and we will insist upon it."

"I have to go now," Emily said. "Miss Alice is expecting me at the library."

"Very well," Miss Browne said. "Emily, I am truly sorry for the pain you feel. But I have the destinies of over a hundred girls in my hands. And they must come first."

Emily gathered both sets of schoolbooks and Mary Kate's letter. "What if you don't find any Hasbroucks?" she asked. "What happens to me then?"

"You'll be sent to another orphanage," Miss Browne said. "Or if none will take you because of your age, you'll go to the poorhouse, in the town you came from."

"I'll run away," Emily said.

"Yes, I expect you will," Miss Browne said. "Good day, Emily."

Emily walked to the library slowly. The two sets of

schoolbooks were heavy. She thought about leaving them behind and running away. How much worse could it be than living with Hasbroucks? They'd probably make her do things no proper girl should.

But she couldn't leave without letting the Webbers know. It wouldn't be right. And besides, the Webbers might decide to adopt her. She wouldn't even have to stay in Oakbridge. She could move in with Miss Alice and Tim when they got married. Something would work out. It just had to.

Emily's mind was on living with Miss Alice and Tim as she entered the library. True, she'd never met Tim, but he must be nice, even if dogs and cats made him sneeze.

"Don't bump into me like that!"

"I'm sorry," Emily said. She looked up and realized it was Harriet she'd bumped into.

"It's bad enough they let you into my school," Harriet said. "How dare you use the library as well?"

"I work here," Emily said. "After school."

"Work is all you're good for," Harriet said. "Wait until my father hears you bumped into me like that."

"Girls," Miss Alice said. "Harriet, you've checked out your books. There's no reason for you to stay here any longer. Emily, I have work for you to do in the back room. Would you go there now?"

"You haven't heard the last of this," Harriet said.

Emily sighed. She wished that just once she *would* hear the last of something.

Seven

When Emily opened her desk on Thursday, she found a note in it. Scribbled in large handwriting on a piece of school paper was the message GET OUT OF TOWN.

Emily wondered who had left it there. Harriet, probably, or Isabella, or Florrie. They were the obvious suspects. But it could have been an Austen girl, or the local police, or even Miss Browne. In spite of herself, Emily smiled.

By the time she waited for Constance at the end of the school day, she had long forgotten about the note. She had spent considerably less time than usual peeking into the classroom that day. Mostly she had sat at her desk, half listening to the lessons, half daydreaming about meeting Constance's family. She didn't even mind losing the twenty-five cents she ordinarily would have earned from working at the library. A real supper with a real family.

Emily had convinced Miss Bessie that morning that she should be allowed to wear her middy dress, which was her Sunday going-to-church dress. She only wished her hair was long enough for a big bow, but it would be soon enough.

"My mother isn't much of a cook," Constance said to Emily as they walked through town. "And we have a terrible time keeping servants. Right now we don't have any, and the house is an awful mess. I don't know what we'll have for supper."

Emily looked at Constance. The two girls had eaten lunch together every day for a week. This was the first time Emily had seen Constance worried.

"It doesn't matter," she said. "I'm not very fussy."

"But you're always so neat," Constance said. "No one in my family is neat."

"It's easier if you have servants," Emily said. She knew what a help Mrs. Macdonald was to the Webbers. "Why do you have terrible trouble keeping one?"

"My father doesn't like them," Constance said. "On account of his being a union man. They make him nervous. And when we get one he can get along with, my mother tries to convince her she should be on the barricades fighting for the vote. Sometimes she even tells the women about birth control." Constance shuddered. "Parents can be a fearsome burden sometimes," she said.

"I wouldn't know," Emily said.

"Oh, I'm sorry," Constance said. "That was awful of me."

"No," Emily said. "It was awful of me. I had a father. I lived with him until I was eight." She thought about her father for a moment. He was a Hasbrouck through and through, but sometimes he'd been kind to her. He'd taught her how to play the piano, and he used to listen to her when she read from her schoolbooks. But mostly he drank. "You're right," she said. "Parents can be a fearsome burden."

"I just don't want you to be disappointed," Constance said. "We don't live in a mansion. There'll be books and papers all over the place. And my mother's been known to burn things. Food that is. But at least she won't be in jail. I made her absolutely promise she wouldn't do anything today to get thrown into jail. I wanted you to meet her."

"That was very nice of you," Emily said. Her father had spent a few nights in jail. All Hasbroucks had, she'd been told. But she doubted it was for anything noble like fighting to give women the right to vote.

"I've never brought a friend over," Constance said. "Not since I was little anyway. You're the first real friend I've ever had."

Emily thought about Gracie and Mary Kate. They'd been her first real friends in many years. She remembered how grateful she'd been to them. "You're my third real friend," she said to Constance. "But the other two are gone."

"Tom and Ben have each other," Constance said.

"And besides, boys are different. They can always play baseball together, even if their fathers hate each other. But I've wanted to have a friend for a long time now."

Emily had known at Austen that she was better off than a lot of the girls there. Mary Kate had been a foundling, and Gracie had spent years waiting for her mother to return. Emily had had a mother and a father and an aunt Mabel to take care of her until she was nearly twelve. But it had never occurred to her that a girl with a real family could be unhappy. "I'm glad we're friends," she said. "And I'm sure I'll like your family."

"If you don't . . . ," Constance began. "Well, if you don't, don't think any the worse of me, all right?"

"All right," Emily said, and then they discussed what had happened during school.

"This is it," Constance said when they arrived at her home. "We don't own it. We only rent. Father never knows where the union is going to send him next so there's no point in buying. That's what he says. I wish we owned a house, though. But if we did, I'd wish this wasn't the one."

Emily looked at the house. From the outside it was ramshackle, not at all the way she'd pictured Constance living.

"There's Tom and Ben," Constance said, and her face lit up. Emily saw two boys playing catch. One was tall with dark hair. The other was shorter, with light brown hair and freckles, just like Constance. "I thought you said they were twins," Emily protested.

"They are," Constance said. "They're just not identical. Tom, Ben, meet Emily. Emily, this is my brother Tom and my brother Ben."

Emily suddenly felt very shy. She had no experience talking to boys and had no idea what to say to them.

"It's nice to meet you, Emily," one of the twins said. "I'm Tom, by the way."

"And I'm Ben," the one that looked like Constance said. "We're glad Connie brought home a friend of hers. Thank you for coming."

"Would you like to play catch?" Tom asked. "Connie plays with us all the time."

"Not today," Constance said. "I want Emily to meet Father and Mother."

"They're both inside," Tom said. "We'll join you there in a while."

"They're so nice," Emily whispered to Constance as they entered the house.

Constance nodded. "They're the nicest boys in the world," she said. "Mother! Father! We're here."

A woman who looked just like Constance came out of the kitchen. She had on a shirtwaist, not unlike the kind Miss Alice wore, but she was wearing an apron over it, and her hair was straggly, falling out of its bun. "Hello, darling," she said to Constance, who walked over and gave her a kiss. "And this must be Emily."

"Yes, ma'am," Emily said. For a moment she couldn't recall what Constance's last name was. But then she remembered. "Hello, Mrs. Crawford."

"I'm so glad you could come," Mrs. Crawford said. "Constance has been looking forward to it so much. Please, put your books down and make yourself comfortable."

Emily looked at the parlor. It was just as Constance had described it, books and papers all over the furniture and floor.

Mrs. Crawford laughed. "Put them down anywhere," she said. "Connie, darling, I know I promised to straighten things up today, but there was an unexpected crisis. Well, I suppose all crises are unexpected. Anyway I had to leave home to attend to some business, which of course took much longer than it should have, and that's why the house looks this way. But at least I didn't get arrested. Tell me, Emily, what are your views on women's suffrage?"

Aunt Mabel had been fiercely opposed to women's voting, Emily knew, and Miss Alice was equally fierce in her support. But nobody had ever cared what her opinion was. Now that she thought about it, nobody had ever cared what her opinion was on anything. "I'd like to be able to vote," she said. "When I grow up, that is."

"And you will be able to, I'm sure of it," Mrs. Crawford said. "I keep telling Connie that she should be the first woman president, but she says she has no interest in politics. Connie, go rouse your father, and I'll go back to the kitchen."

Constance left the room. Emily felt nervous again, being alone with Mrs. Crawford.

"I suppose Connie's already warned you about my cooking," Mrs. Crawford said.

"I'm looking forward to supper anyway," Emily said. "I mean, I'm sure supper will be just fine."

Mrs. Crawford laughed. "It will be wonderful," she said. "I can promise you that because I didn't cook it. My friend's cook prepared a chicken for us. We'll have it cold, so there's no chance I'll burn it. I hope cold chicken is satisfactory, Emily."

Emily had never had chicken on a weekday before. "It sounds wonderful," she said.

"I agree," Mrs. Crawford said. "It's so nice to meet you, Emily. Connie has told us so many wonderful things about you. And she goes on so about your hair. I swear that girl is going to take a pair of scissors to her hair someday just to have it short like yours."

"I'd like mine to be longer," Emily said. "I'd like to have a pretty bow to wear in it."

"My hair never does what it's supposed to," Mrs. Crawford said. "If short hair were acceptable, I think I'd cut mine as well. But men make the rules of fashion, and men do like long hair. Oh, well. When women get the vote, all such things will change. It will be a wonderful time then, Emily. Perhaps by the time you're old enough to vote, you'll be able to. Wouldn't that be a wonder?"

"It certainly would, ma'am," Emily said.

"And perhaps by the time she's ready to work, this will be a worker's utopia," a man said. He was walking hand in hand with Constance, so Emily was sure it was her father. "I'm Hank Crawford," he said. "I'm pleased to meet you, Emily."

Mr. Crawford looked just like his son Tom. Emily wondered what it must feel like to belong to a family where you knew who you looked like. She thought it must be splendid.

"A worker's paradise and a woman president," Mrs. Crawford said. "And all by the time Emily is twenty-one. I hope we're not promising too much."

"That's all right," Emily said. "I like those promises."

"That's because they're good ones," Mr. Crawford said. "Even though they'll take a lot of hard work and sacrifice to achieve."

"Oh, Father," Constance said. "Can't the revolution wait until after supper?"

Emily was terrified the Crawfords would get angry at the outburst. To her surprise, they merely laughed.

"Why don't you and Emily go to your room and visit for a while?" Mrs. Crawford suggested. "You might do your schoolwork. That way when supper and the revolution come, you'll have it done already."

Constance and Emily left the parlor and went to Constance's bedroom. Emily continued to marvel at the

71

Crawfords and how they looked alike and didn't get angry when Constance spoke back to them. Emily never would have dared to say such a thing. "Your parents are so wonderful," she said when they were alone in Constance's room. "They're as wonderful as your brothers."

"I suppose," Constance said. "I just wish sometimes they'd put the revolution aside for a bit and be more normal. I know they try, but when you rent your home, it just isn't the same. This isn't at all how I'd like my bedroom to be."

Emily looked the room over. It wasn't very large, and the furniture looked worn. Unlike the parlor, though, it was neat. There was a real bed, a real desk and chair, a chest of drawers, a bookcase, a rag rug on the floor, and curtains on the bed. And there was no sampler on the wall proclaiming that the wages of sin is death. Emily had awakened to that sampler every morning she'd lived with Aunt Mabel.

Emily thought about telling Constance what a wonderful room she had, but she decided against it. She'd already told her she had wonderful brothers and parents. She didn't need to hear that her rented bedroom was wonderful as well. "How would you like it?" Emily asked instead.

"I'd like a big bay window," Constance said. "Overlooking a cherry tree. We had a cherry tree three houses back, and in the springtime it was the most beautiful thing I've ever seen. And in my bedroom, I want a canopy bed with a real lace coverlet and curtains to match. And no rag rug. Something pretty on the floor. And the furniture should all be cherry wood, and the desk should be pretty, not some hand-me-down that's all nicked and marked up. And I'd like the room to be yellow. Yellow's my favorite color. Mother says when I'm grown up I can have a bedroom just like that, but Mother says when I'm grown up I can be president, and I don't think that's going to happen either. What's your room like?"

"I don't have one," Emily said. "I'm sleeping in the spare room at the Webbers'."

"Father says I should be grateful for what I have," Constance said. "He says the mill families, the people who work for Mr. Sheldon and men like that, they live in terrible poverty. The company owns their houses, and most of the families live in two or three rooms. In the winter the houses are cold as ice, and in the summer you could melt from the heat. He says when the times are good, if there aren't too many in the family, they have enough to eat. But when times are bad, the mill-hands are let go, and their families are lucky not to starve. And that if there's an accident, and the worker gets hurt, then he loses his salary, and they're evicted and end up in the poorhouse."

"That's terrible," Emily said.

"It is," Constance said. "But I still wish I had a canopy bed. What would you like your bedroom to look like?"

Like this one, Emily thought. In a house filled with brothers and parents and piles of books and papers. "I don't know," she said. "I guess I never thought about it."

"I promise that you won't always live in a spare room," Constance said. "I promise you someday you'll have a room all your own. A real bedroom just the way you want it."

"And I promise you someday you'll be president," Emily said, and she and Constance burst into wild howls of laughter.

Eight

Tuesday morning, Emily sat at her desk in the hallway and discovered she was happy. It came almost as a surprise to her. But when she thought about it, she realized she had a lot to feel happy about.

Life had settled into a pleasant routine with the Webbers, and nobody had said anything about her moving out. She had begun piano lessons with Mrs. Bell on Saturday and had spent every spare moment practicing her assignments on the Webbers' piano. The previous night she'd had supper again with Constance and her family. This time no one else's cook had prepared the meal, and the food was almost as bad as Constance had predicted. But it didn't matter. The Crawfords had argued and teased and laughed and even included Emily in some of their jokes. And Mrs. Crawford had said that the next time Emily came over, she had to bring Aunt Bessie and Miss Alice with her. That thought alone was enough to make Emily happy.

But the best part was Emily's hair. It had been growing out steadily, and Emily knew that in a couple of weeks it would be long enough for a bow. Aunt Bessie had promised they'd go shopping for one as soon as Emily was ready. "I can't get over what a pretty girl you are," Aunt Bessie had declared just that morning. "You have a smile that lights up the heavens."

Emily wasn't so sure about that, but she smiled at the thought. She knew nothing good lasted forever, or even very long, but that didn't mean she couldn't enjoy it while it was happening.

"Now, class, take out your geography books," she heard Mrs. Hearst say.

Emily wondered if Miss Upshaw would ever relent and let her back into the classroom. She knew her grades would be better if she could see and hear things more clearly. Then she shook her head. Why let thoughts of Miss Upshaw disturb such a pleasant morning?

She opened her desk to get her geography book and screamed. There was something horrible in the desk. It took her a moment to realize it was a dead bird. Someone had put a dead bird in her desk.

Emily didn't allow herself the luxury of thought. She took out her pretty new handkerchief and used it to pick up the bird. Then she marched into Mrs. Hearst's classroom.

"Emily, are you all right?" Mrs. Hearst asked, but Emily ignored her. When she knew she was close enough not to miss, she flung the bird at the person she knew must have left it. "Murderer!" she screamed at Harriet, feeling close to ecstasy at the power of the word and the accuracy of her throw.

Harriet screamed even before the bird hit her, but once it did she became hysterical. She jumped up and started waving her arms around as though to brush off any remnants of the bird. Emily laughed at her gyrations. That got Isabella and Florrie going. They began to cry while Harriet maintained her hysterical dance.

Miss Upshaw stormed into the classroom, walked straight over to Emily, and slapped her hard across the face. Emily gasped, both at the pain and at the injustice. If Miss Upshaw had not then grabbed her by the arms to shake her, Emily would have hit her back.

"Miss Upshaw!" Mrs. Hearst said. "Stop it!"

But there seemed to be no stopping the principal, who continued shaking Emily with all her might. Emily, in a state of terror and rage, kicked Miss Upshaw sharply in her shin. Miss Upshaw responded by hitting Emily so hard with the back of her hand that Emily fell to the floor.

Mrs. Hearst ran toward Emily and pulled her away. "Charles, get the nurse," she said. "Now!"

A boy ran out of the classroom. Emily could see from the floor that Harriet was still screaming and gyrating, and Isabella and Florrie were still crying. Miss Upshaw's face was scarlet.

"Give her to me now," Miss Upshaw said to Mrs. Hearst. "Or I'll have your job."

"No," Mrs. Hearst said. "Emily, stand behind me."

Emily got up and did as Mrs. Hearst said. Fear and anger were raging their own battle inside her. She yearned to pummel them all with her fists, batter Harriet, Isabella, and Florrie until they lay bleeding on the floor. And she felt an equally strong desire to punch Miss Upshaw in her stomach, make her gasp for breath, and then punch her again and again.

Miss Upshaw took a couple of steps toward her. The rest of the class was in a state of pandemonium. Several of the children had begun crying for no reason that Emily could see. Two other teachers had come into the classroom.

"Give that girl to me," Miss Upshaw said. "No child will kick me and get away with it."

"Mrs. Davis, call Alice Webber at the library," Mrs. Hearst said. "Tell her to come here immediately." A teacher ran out of the room.

"Miss Upshaw, you are not going to hurt this child anymore," Mrs. Hearst said.

"I am in charge of disciplining the children," Miss Upshaw said. "And that's not a child you're protecting. It's a wild animal. Now, give her to me."

"Leave her alone," Constance said. "You're just a big bully. And an oppressor of the masses."

The school nurse ran into the classroom and was confronted by a scene of total chaos. She walked over to Harriet first and gave her a nervous slap across the face.

Harriet screamed once more and then collapsed into tears.

"How dare you hit that child?" Miss Upshaw asked. "Don't you know who she is?"

"She was in hysterics," the nurse said. "And I hardly touched her. What's going on here?"

"Emily threw a dead bird at Harriet," one of the girls said.

"She put it in my desk," Emily said. "I just threw it back at her."

"And Emily called her a murderer," another girl said.

Emily could see the whole classroom from where she was standing. Most of the kids who had been crying had stopped, even Florrie, who seemed interested in what was going to happen next. The Austen girls, sitting in their back row, all looked terror-stricken.

"Has anybody here been hurt?" the nurse asked.

"Emily," Mrs. Hearst said. "Miss Upshaw shook her within an inch of her life and hit her hard enough to knock her to the floor."

"I did what I had to do," Miss Upshaw said. "And I'll do more once I get my hands on that miserable creature."

The nurse walked over to Emily. "You're going to have quite a black eye," she said. She took Emily's wrist in her hand and held it lightly. "And your heart is racing," she said. "A pulse of a hundred and twenty. Emily, come with me to my office and I'll tend to you."

"No," Miss Upshaw said. "She attacked Harriet Dale. She kicked me. I intend to paddle her as punishment and then throw her out of this school myself."

"I'm sorry, Miss Upshaw," the nurse said. "But the physical care of the children is my responsibility. And no matter who did what to whom, this child needs medical attention. Mrs. Hearst, have the girl's mother sent for."

"I've already taken care of that," Mrs. Hearst replied. "Emily, go with Nurse Kane. I'll have Miss Webber meet you there."

Emily started to shake. She didn't know if she could walk past Miss Upshaw. She was sure the principal would grab her and beat her.

Nurse Kane took Emily and led her gently out of the room. Emily tried not to look at Miss Upshaw or at Harriet. The other children had calmed down, and Emily could feel their eyes on her as she walked out of the room.

It was comforting to be in the nurse's office. Nurse Kane put a blanket around her and washed her face gently. Emily cried out when Nurse Kane treated her cuts and bruises, but the pain subsided and she felt able to breathe more easily.

"What happened?" Miss Alice cried when she arrived at the office. "Oh my God, Emily. Who did this to you?"

"Miss Upshaw," Nurse Kane said.

"Why?" Miss Alice asked. "Who would do that to a child?"

"I don't know exactly what happened," Nurse Kane said. "Mrs. Hearst probably does. I'll send for her right away."

Miss Alice held Emily in her arms. "It'll be all right," she murmured. "We'll take care of it."

Emily had refused to cry, but it was hard not to, with Miss Alice there. A few minutes later both Mrs. Hearst and Miss Upshaw came to the nurse's office.

"Miss Upshaw, how dare you attack this child?" Miss Alice said as the principal walked in.

"I was well within my rights," Miss Upshaw said. "She brutalized Harriet Dale, terrified that poor child with a vicious physical attack. And then she turned on me. No child has ever struck me before, and this one will not get away with it."

Mrs. Hearst walked over to Emily. "Emily, where did that bird come from?" she asked. "And why did you throw it at Harriet?"

"It was in my desk," Emily said. "Somebody left it there. I'm sure it was Harriet."

"Nonsense," Miss Upshaw said. "You brought it to school for the express purpose of frightening Harriet. That's exactly the sort of filthy behavior we've all come to expect from you."

"No," Emily said. "I found it. Somebody put it in my desk."

"Was that why you screamed?" Mrs. Hearst asked. "We heard you scream in the hallway."

"I opened my desk and there it was," Emily said.

"Remember, you told us to take out our geography books."

"And then you ran into the classroom," Mrs. Hearst said. "You found the bird in the hallway, you screamed, you ran into the classroom, and you threw the bird at Harriet."

"There's something I don't understand," Miss Alice said. "What was Emily doing in the hallway?"

The others turned to her. "Emily never told you?" Mrs. Hearst asked.

"Told me what?" Miss Alice said.

"Miss Upshaw decided Emily couldn't stay in the classroom," Mrs. Hearst said. "She's been taking classes from the hallway since the first day she came back."

"I don't believe this," Miss Alice said. "Miss Upshaw, are you mad?"

"I don't need to hear that from you or anyone else," Miss Upshaw said. "Emily Hasbrouck has caused nothing but trouble since her first day here. And now she's been violent to both Harriet Dale and myself, and you're acting as though I were to blame."

Mrs. Hearst ignored her. "Emily, do you know for a fact that Harriet put the bird in your desk?" she asked.

Emily shook her head. "But it's just the kind of thing she would do," she said. "Half the time when she walks in the hallway, she kicks me under the desk. And she is a murderer. She killed Gracie."

"There's that slander again," Miss Upshaw said. "As

though a fine girl like Harriet Dale would ever dirty her hands with one of those Austen creatures."

"There's nothing fine about Harriet Dale," Mrs. Hearst said. "Or Isabella Cosgrove or Florrie Sheldon either, for that matter. They're nasty and cruel, and frankly, the way they've been behaving ever since Emily came back to school, I suspect they're feeling guilty about something."

"About killing Gracie," Emily said, although she doubted that any of them was capable of feeling guilt.

"Mrs. Hearst, I've warned you once already that I will have your job if you persist with these lies," Miss Upshaw said. "There's one bad apple in your classroom and that's Emily Hasbrouck. She represents the worst of the Austen wards, and none of them are any too good, coming as they do from the dregs of society. And to think that you might take the word of one of them over that of Harriet Dale or Isabella Cosgrove. Girls born into the best families of Oakbridge, of this entire state. Girls with breeding. Your attitude is disgraceful, and I am seriously considering having the school board fire you."

"No," Emily said. "Please. It's not her fault. Mrs. Hearst was just being nice to me. Because she's kind. That's all. She's a wonderful teacher. Don't fire her."

"And why should I listen to you?" Miss Upshaw asked. "A filthy, disgusting guttersnipe?"

"I'm sorry," Emily said, and she could feel the tears

streaming down her face. "It's all my fault. I was just so sure it was Harriet who put the bird in my desk."

"So you're persisting in that lie," Miss Upshaw said. "You refuse to admit you were the one who brought the dead bird to school."

"I didn't," Emily said. "Somebody left it there. Honest."

"You don't know the meaning of the word *honest*," Miss Upshaw said. "Any more than you know gratitude or humility. And until you do learn just what those words mean, I will not have you in attendance here."

"And what kind of threat is that?" Miss Alice asked.

"Emily Hasbrouck is suspended," Miss Upshaw said. "And I intend to see to it that she is expelled from this school. I will also call Miss Browne and determine a placement at an orphanage or poorhouse more suited for such a creature. And that is not a hollow threat, Miss Webber. I feel I must warn you, if you choose to defend her in any way, the Dales and the Cosgroves and the Sheldons will see to it you no longer work at the library. And you too, Mrs. Hearst, will find yourself without employment. These are powerful people, and they will protect their daughters at any cost."

"I'll take my chances," Miss Alice said. "Emily can't be expelled without a full school board hearing. I investigated that when she came back to Oakbridge. And I'll see to it the school board hears all about how you've been persecuting Emily from her first day here. And not just Emily, but all the Austen girls."

Miss Upshaw laughed. "Mr. Sheldon is on the school board," she said. "As is Mayor Dale. Judge Cosgrove is the school board president. Do you really think Emily stands a chance?"

"The truth will out," Miss Alice said. "Come on, Emily. We're going home. You'll be safe there. I promise."

Nine

The last time Emily had seen so many adults crammed into one parlor had been after her aunt Mabel's funeral. Then, as now, the topic of Emily's future had been on everyone's minds. But now, Emily told herself, all the adults were on her side.

It was the day after the incident with the bird, and the night before Emily's expulsion hearing. Miss Upshaw had requested an emergency school board meeting to deal with the situation, and the board had wasted no time setting a date.

"That's not a good sign," Mr. Crawford said as he sat on Aunt Bessie's horsehair couch. "They're giving us no time to prepare a defense."

Emily looked around the room. Aunt Bessie and Miss Alice both looked grave. Mrs. Crawford looked angry. Mrs. Hearst looked pained. Tom and Ben looked uncomfortable. And Constance looked worried.

"They won't send Emily away, will they, Father?" she asked.

"That will be Miss Browne's decision," he replied. "This whole situation is really a disgrace. If Miss Browne buckles under the coercion, she'll feel compelled to find someplace else for Emily to live."

"Even if she doesn't, and Emily is expelled, I don't know what we'll do," Miss Alice said. "Mother and I both work. We can't look after her when she should be in school."

"I don't need looking after," Emily said.

"But you do need schooling," Aunt Bessie said. "And there's no other school to send you to."

"If only you hadn't thrown that bird at Harriet," Mrs. Hearst said.

"She deserved it," Constance said. "Father, she really is dreadful. She's cruel to everyone she doesn't think is as good as she is."

"Miss Browne said I'd have to go to the poorhouse," Emily said. "There's one in the town I used to live in."

"When did she tell you that?" Aunt Bessie asked.

"Last week sometime," Emily said. "She sent for me from school."

Aunt Bessie shook her head in disgust. "I know she's a friend of yours, Alice," she said. "But what a thing to threaten a child with."

"She's in a terrible situation, Mother," Miss Alice said. "I've seen her in tears over all this. She's doing all she can to save the Austen Home, and she feels if Emily must be sacrificed, then so be it."

"What can we do to see that Emily is not sacrificed?"

Mrs. Crawford asked. "I assume if Emily isn't expelled, if the school board can be made to see reason, then you, Mrs. Webber, will let Emily stay with you?"

"Emily's welcome here for as long as it takes," Aunt Bessie replied. "I love having her stay with us."

"If she isn't expelled, Miss Browne must be made to see reason," Mr. Crawford said. "Emily can hardly be thrown into the poorhouse when she's committed no crime."

"None of this will be easy," Mrs. Hearst declared. "Miss Upshaw remains outraged. If Emily does return to school, I don't want to think of how Miss Upshaw will respond."

"She'll respond the way the law makes her respond," Mr. Crawford said. "Her attack on Emily falls just short of criminal assault."

"I don't want Mrs. Hearst to lose her job," Emily said. "Or Miss Alice. But I don't want to go to the poorhouse either."

"There are seven members of the school board," Mr. Crawford said. "Of course the odds would be better if there were nine. But if four of them see reason, then Emily won't be expelled."

"I think we can count on Reverend Jones," Miss Alice said. "I spoke to him yesterday and told him of the whole situation."

"And I've spoken to Mr. Schmidt," Mrs. Crawford said. "A fine man. Very sympathetic to suffrage. He promised not to prejudge the situation, but to listen with an open mind to all Emily and Mrs. Hearst had to say."

"That's a possible two votes," Aunt Bessie said.

"I think we'll be able to count on Mr. Thompkins," Mrs. Hearst said. "His wife is a dear friend of mine, and I've spoken of Emily's situation to her in the past."

"Then we have a good chance at three votes for Emily," Mr. Crawford said. "But we certainly must count on three votes against as well. What of the seventh board member?"

"Mr. Keller," Miss Alice said. "He'll never oppose Judge Cosgrove."

"Roger Keller, the lawyer?" Mr. Crawford asked. Miss Alice nodded. "I suspect you're right," he said. "He's an ambitious man. He'll never go against what the powerful forces insist upon."

"What are you saying?" Constance asked. "That Emily's going to be thrown out of school, out of Oakbridge, because no one has the courage to stand up against those men?"

"This is an unjust world," her father replied. "We must fight clean and hard, but we shouldn't assume a happy outcome."

"I can apologize for throwing the bird at Harriet," Emily said. "And for kicking Miss Upshaw. Even though they both deserved it. Would that help?"

"I don't think that would be enough," Mrs. Hearst

said. "I'm sorry, Emily, but I don't think the Dales and the Cosgroves and the Sheldons will rest until you're out of town."

"That's because I know they killed Gracie," Emily said. "But even if they throw me into the poorhouse, I'll make them pay for that."

"They're paying already, if that's any comfort," Mrs. Hearst said. "Isabella Cosgrove is close to a breakdown. And Harriet yesterday—I've never seen a child possessed that way. Poor Florrie. Yes, I know you don't like her and hold her responsible, but that child is treated close to an outcast by her family because she's crippled. And I've heard rumors that her family is planning to send her away because her imperfections bother them so. A scandal like this is just what they dread."

"They deserve everything they get and more," Constance said. "Isabella can have a breakdown at some fine sanitarium. And Florrie won't be sent to a poorhouse. Father, if Emily is forced to leave Oakbridge, then I'm leaving too. She's the only friend I've ever had. I'll move into the poorhouse with her."

"That's a lovely sentiment," her mother said. "And we'll miss you if you do. But meanwhile, let's try to keep that from happening."

There was a knock on the door. "Do you know who that might be?" Mr. Crawford asked.

Miss Alice shook her head.

"Be careful," he said.

"I'm sure there's nothing to worry about," she replied. She opened the door and found Miss Browne standing there.

"I have wonderful news," Miss Browne said.

"Come in," Miss Alice said. "We can all use some wonderful news."

Miss Browne walked into the parlor. She seemed surprised to see so many people there. "I've found a way out of all this," she said. "It took a great deal of searching, but I found a member of the Hasbrouck family willing to let Emily live with him."

"What?" Miss Alice asked.

Miss Browne looked excited. "It took many telephone calls," she said. "And quite a bit of letter writing. Emily, your father has some family left, but most of them would have nothing to do with you. I told them of your plight, and they turned a deaf ear."

"I told you," Emily said. "Aunt Mabel always said they were no good."

"But just this evening, I spoke to one who was quite different," Miss Browne said. "He's your uncle, Emily. Did you even know you had an uncle?"

Emily shook her head. "Father never mentioned a brother."

"I admit I don't know much about him," Miss Browne said. "And under ordinary circumstances, I would investigate him most thoroughly before releasing any of my girls into the care of a stranger. But these circumstances are hardly ordinary. He agreed it was his moral responsibility to look after his brother's orphaned child, and said he would arrange to take her from Oak-bridge within the next few weeks."

"You can't do that," Aunt Bessie said. "You can't just ship Emily out of here without at least meeting this man first. How much contact have you had with him?"

Miss Browne blushed. "Just a few minutes on the telephone this evening," she admitted. "Mrs. Webber, you have no idea how frustrating it's been to speak to relative after relative of Emily's, only to have them refuse to accept her. Aunts, cousins, other uncles. There seem to be countless Hasbroucks, and all of them drunkards or worse. Emily was most fortunate to have her aunt Mabel to care for her. But this one Mr. Has-brouck, an older brother of Emily's father, sounded quite respectable. He's married and has children of his own, and as soon as he heard that Emily was homeless, he offered her his home. We should thank the good Lord that Emily has such an uncle, and not worry that his motives are less than pure."

"I won't let Emily move in with a stranger," Aunt Bessie said.

"We have no choice," Miss Browne said. "Emily must leave Oakbridge if we are to salvage any of this wretched situation."

"If Mr. Hasbrouck is a decent man, then of course we'll be happy to let Emily move in with him," Miss Alice said. "Mother, you know all along we've wanted Emily to have a real home. Not just a bed in our spare room. Won't that be wonderful for you, Emily? You'll be living with family again."

"But they're Hasbroucks," Emily said. "Aunt Mabel said all Hasbroucks are derelicts and sinners."

"Let us pray Aunt Mabel was wrong," Miss Browne said.

"Forgive me for interrupting," Mr. Crawford said. "But should we cancel Emily's expulsion hearing? If she leaves Oakbridge, that should satisfy the Dales and the others."

Miss Browne looked ill at ease. "I'm afraid we must go through with it," she said. "I spoke to Mayor Dale before coming here. I thought if he heard about Mr. Hasbrouck's kind offer, that would be enough for him. But he insisted on going through with the hearing. He wants the expulsion on Emily's permanent record."

"What a cruel man," Mrs. Crawford said.

"Well, Emily did throw a dead bird at his daughter," Miss Browne said. "And he says Harriet is a delicate child, easily upset."

Constance snorted. "Harriet's as delicate as a cobra."

"It's all settled, then, isn't it?" Emily said. "I'll be sent to live with Mr. Hasbrouck, no matter what sort of man he is. Even if he lets me go to school, they'll think of me as a troublemaker, someone expelled from her previous school. And no one will ever admit the truth about how Gracie died."

"I know it seems bad to you now," Miss Browne said. "But God works in mysterious—"

She never had the chance to finish her thought. There was a sound of shattering glass, and a sudden cry from Aunt Bessie.

Emily didn't know what had happened. At first she thought that a mirror had fallen off a wall. But she quickly saw that the parlor window had smashed into a thousand little pieces and Aunt Bessie was lying on the floor, her head bleeding profusely.

Mrs. Crawford raced to Aunt Bessie's side. "Someone call for a doctor!" she cried. "Tom, Ben, go outside and catch whoever did this."

Mrs. Hearst raced to the telephone. The boys ran outside.

"It's a rock," Miss Alice said. "Someone threw a rock through our window. Mother? Mother, are you all right?"

"She's lost consciousness," Mrs. Crawford said. "We must bandage the wound. Quick, someone, get me towels and hot water."

Emily had stood when the rock came crashing through the window, but now she found herself unable to move. All she could think of was Gracie, killed when her head hit a rock. Was Aunt Bessie going to die the same way? And would she, Emily, again be responsible for the death of someone who cared for her?

There was a mad rush at the front door as first Dr. Edwards appeared, followed shortly by Tom, Ben, and a strange boy. Dr. Edwards had been the doctor who had declared Gracie dead, and Emily began to sob at the very sight of him. But under his ministrations, Aunt Bessie began to moan, and shortly thereafter to speak.

"What happened?" she asked.

"Quiet, Mother," Miss Alice said. "Don't upset yourself."

"Let's move her onto this couch," Dr. Edwards said. He and Mr. Crawford lifted Aunt Bessie and gently put her on the sofa. "You'll be fine, Mrs. Webber," the doctor said. "Just a glancing blow, really. You were very lucky."

"This boy threw the rock," Tom said.

"Three people saw him running away from the front yard," Ben added.

Mr. Crawford walked over to the boy. "Who are you?" he asked. "And why did you throw a rock through the window?"

"I ain't talking," the boy said.

"I know him," Mrs. Hearst said. "He's a fourth-grader at our school. John Winston. John, you're a good boy. Whatever possessed you to do such a thing?"

"You could have killed my mother," Miss Alice said. "This is not a childish prank."

"Speak up, boy," Mr. Crawford said. "Why did you throw the rock?"

"Because I didn't want her back at school," the boy said. "She doesn't belong here. Not with decent people. Why doesn't she just leave and let us get on with our lives?"

"Did Harriet Dale make you throw the rock?" Constance asked. "Or Isabella Cosgrove or Florrie Sheldon?"

"None of them," the boy said. "They didn't have to. Everyone in this town hates her. I just did what everyone else wants to do. I'm sorry the rock hit somebody else. I didn't mean to hit that old lady. But I'm not sorry I threw it. You hear me? I'm not sorry at all."

"You'll be sorry when your parents hear about it," Mr. Crawford said. "I can promise you that."

"You ain't taking me home," the boy said.

"Either I am or the police are," Mr. Crawford said. "It's your choice, boy. Which will it be?"

"The police don't scare me," the boy said. "They want her out of town too."

"It doesn't matter what they want," Mr. Crawford said. "You threw a rock through a window and hurt Bessie Webber, a respected member of this community. And several people saw you running away from here, and even more have heard you confess. I can talk to either your parents or the police. I suggest, for your sake, we start with your parents."

"I'll go with you," Mrs. Hearst said. "I had Johnny's sister in my class last year. I know the family."

"Very well," Mr. Crawford said. "Come, John." He took the boy's elbow and escorted him out of the house.

"This is a terrible thing," Miss Browne said. "Emily, I'm sorry there's so much ill feeling toward you in this town. But you must see now how much better things will be when you live with your uncle."

Emily nodded. She brought nothing but danger and pain to people. Better the Hasbroucks should deal with her cursed existence.

Ten

Emily was shocked at the number of people attending her expulsion hearing. She clung to Aunt Bessie's side as they made their way through the room, past hostile looks and angry whispers.

"Don't you worry," Aunt Bessie said. She wore a bandage on her head but had insisted on attending. Emily knew Aunt Bessie should have stayed home, but she was glad to have such a loving presence to protect her. Miss Alice walked in with Mr. and Mrs. Crawford. They were the people Emily knew she could depend on. Mrs. Hearst might want to protect her, but she had her job to worry about. And Miss Browne put the Austen Home and its needs first. Emily had the Webbers and the Crawfords and that was all.

She sat in the front row and remembered again Aunt Mabel's funeral. She'd been a front-row mourner then as well. Only now people weren't whispering "Poor child." They were condemning her instead.

The members of the school board sat at a long table

in the front of the room. Seven distinguished-looking gentlemen. It startled Emily to realize three of them were the fathers of the girls who had caused all this trouble. Judge Cosgrove sat in the center, since he was president of the board. She recognized Mayor Dale from his picture in the newspaper. She had seen it there often enough. She asked Mr. Crawford which one was Mr. Sheldon, and he pointed him out to her, along with Mr. Keller. Reverend Jones wore a clerical collar, and Mrs. Crawford exchanged a brief wave with a man Emily assumed was Mr. Schmidt. That left the unidentified man as Mr. Thompkins.

Emily tried not to worry. So what if she was expelled? If Miss Browne had her way, she'd be expelled from the entire community of Oakbridge anyway. But she knew whatever this Hasbrouck relative of hers was like, expulsion was a serious problem. If he took on her guardianship convinced she was a bad girl, more trouble than she was worth, he would be more likely to mistreat her, or throw her out of his home. Or he might reject the idea of taking her in at all, and then Emily would have to face the very real possibility of the poorhouse.

It was all Aunt Mabel's fault, Emily suddenly decided. She should never have gone on and on about what an honor it was to be a Lathrop. It wasn't as though she'd treated Emily like one. She'd told her repeatedly she was half Hasbrouck and thus one step away from eternal damnation. And when she'd gotten ill, Emily had been made to leave school and had been turned into nothing better than a servant. Hardly the way a Lathrop should be brought up.

But Emily had only heard the part about how Lathrops were upstanding members of the community and deserved to be treated as such. So she resented being in an orphanage, and worse yet had stood up to Harriet and the others, demanding they treat her as their equal. If she had allowed them the pleasure of their petty humiliations from the beginning, then they would have tired of her and treated her no differently than they treated the other Austen girls, with contempt but little physical cruelty.

"This meeting will now come to order," Judge Cosgrove proclaimed. "This is a special meeting of the school board of Oakbridge to determine whether Emily Hasbrouck, a sixth-grader, should be expelled from the Oakbridge Primary School. If you are here, Emily Hasbrouck, stand up."

Emily stood. Her back was to everyone except the school board members, but she could feel a hundred pairs of eyes on her anyway.

Mr. Crawford stood up at the same time. "I'm here to represent Emily," he said.

"I wasn't aware she needed legal representation," Judge Cosgrove said. "This is purely an academic matter."

"It's hardly that," Mr. Crawford said. "Emily Hasbrouck has been the victim of verbal and physical abuse.

An eleven-year-old child needs legal protection to guarantee that this pattern of misbehavior will not be continued."

"I don't see how it harms anyone if the child has a lawyer present," Reverend Jones declared. "Why don't we simply proceed and not get caught up by side issues?"

"Very well," Judge Cosgrove said. "But if Mr. Crawford takes undue liberties, he will no longer be permitted to stay."

"I understand," Mr. Crawford answered.

"We'll hear from Miss Upshaw first," Judge Cosgrove said.

Miss Upshaw limped to the front of the room and took a chair by the desk where the board members were sitting. "Emily Hasbrouck attacked me," she began. "She left me with limited use of my left leg. My doctor is uncertain when I will be able to walk again."

"Terrible, terrible," Mayor Dale muttered.

"This attack, I assume, was unprovoked," Mr. Sheldon said.

"It most certainly was," Miss Upshaw replied.

"And was this the first time you've had trouble with the Hasbrouck girl?" Mayor Dale asked.

"Absolutely not," Miss Upshaw answered. "From the moment Emily Hasbrouck set foot in my school she has caused nothing but trouble. She is a notorious bully. The very day she started at my school, she viciously

101

attacked Harriet Dale, Isabella Cosgrove, and poor Florrie Sheldon. And what was worse, she instigated other Austen girls to do the same. It is a terrible struggle for us at the school to maintain order with the Austen girls. They intimidate the other children with their ill manners and their vulgar tongues. Austen girls are punished at three times the rate of other children at the school. Miss Browne and I have regular conversations about the importance of teaching the Austen girls to be grateful for the charity the good people of this town bestow upon them. But it takes only one bad girl, such as Emily Hasbrouck, to disturb the order we try so hard to maintain. If she is allowed to stay in school any longer, then the other Austen girls will rise up and attack the good children of this town. You wait and see. That is just what will happen."

"That's not true!" Emily cried.

"Silence!" Judge Cosgrove said. "You'll speak when we tell you to."

"Miss Upshaw, what particular incident occurred the other day?" Mayor Dale asked. "Or did Emily Hasbrouck merely attack you unprovoked?"

"She was quite mad," Miss Upshaw said. "She brought a dead bird into the school and flung it at your daughter, Mayor Dale. Poor Harriet naturally cried out in terror, and I, upon hearing the noise, went to Mrs. Hearst's classroom to see what was happening. As soon as Emily Hasbrouck saw me, she began punching and kicking me. Of course I was glad she was no longer focusing her madness upon Harriet, but still she did grievous bodily harm to me. She is a danger to society. We cannot possibly allow her back in our school again."

"Miss Upshaw, we are very grateful to you for leaving your sickbed to address us this evening," Mayor Dale said. "I think you can safely assume you will never have to deal with Emily Hasbrouck again."

"Excuse me," Mr. Crawford said. "Might I ask Miss Upshaw some questions?"

"Very well," Judge Cosgrove said. "But be brief."

"Miss Upshaw, do you see Emily Hasbrouck in this room?" Mr. Crawford asked.

"Unfortunately, I do," Miss Upshaw replied.

"Does her face appear bruised?" Mr. Crawford asked.

"It might be," Miss Upshaw said. "The light is not particularly good."

"Emily, please walk over to Miss Upshaw," Mr. Crawford gently ordered. Emily did as she was told, although she yearned to stay in her seat. "Now," he said. "Can you see bruises on Emily's face?"

"Perhaps," Miss Upshaw said. "Certainly nothing serious."

"Emily, turn around so the members of the school board can see your face," Mr. Crawford said. "Fine. Now come back and sit down. Miss Upshaw, how did Emily get the black eye, for example? How did she get those bruises?"

"I'm certain I don't know," Miss Upshaw answered.

"When you went into the classroom to protect Harriet Dale, was Emily's face bruised then?" Mr. Crawford asked.

"Perhaps," Miss Upshaw said. "Perhaps not. I didn't have much of an opportunity to look at her, since she was beating me so savagely."

"And during this savage attack, did you fight back?" Mr. Crawford asked.

"I might have," Miss Upshaw said. "I feared for my life."

"Is it possible that even before Emily attacked you, you struck her?" Mr. Crawford asked.

"If I did, it was merely to protect Harriet," Miss Upshaw said. "As principal of the school, I have the right to use physical punishment on the children. The Austen girls in particular have often felt the pain of a good paddling."

"But you didn't paddle Emily, did you?" Mr. Crawford said. "There wasn't time. Harriet was screaming, the other children in the room were upset, and you were certain that Emily was the cause of it all just from the sound of voices."

"It was obvious she was the culprit," Miss Upshaw said. "She was standing near Harriet, laughing at her."

"Weren't other children laughing?" Mr. Crawford asked.

"Emily had no business being in the classroom," Miss Upshaw said. "She isn't allowed in the room. Seeing her there proved to me immediately who the troublemaker was. Not that I would have had any doubts anyway."

"Please tell us why Emily wasn't supposed to be in the classroom," Mr. Crawford said.

"Because I allowed her back only on the condition that she took her lessons in the hallway," Miss Upshaw said. "It was the best I could do to protect the other children from her evil ways. She is allowed no association with the other children. Not even the other Austen girls must be infected by her."

"Are you telling us Emily Hasbrouck sits in the hallway at school all day long?" Reverend Jones asked.

"If I had had my way, she never would have been allowed in the school," Miss Upshaw said. "I did what I could to protect the others."

"And so when you saw her in the classroom, you were certain she was causing Harriet's upset," Mr. Crawford said. "So you walked over to Emily, without asking any questions, and struck her."

"I did indeed," Miss Upshaw said.

"But you didn't stop there, did you?" Mr. Crawford pressed on quickly but calmly. "You must have been outraged that for all your efforts to keep Emily from the good girls, she was still attacking them. A paddling wouldn't have sufficed, would it?"

"It was the sight of her laughing," Miss Upshaw said. "It enraged me. I shook Emily as hard as I could simply to make her stop laughing."

"And then Emily kicked you," Mr. Crawford said.

"Once, in the leg. And you, feeling more punishment was in order, hit Emily so hard you blacked her eye and sent her halfway across the classroom. Is that not correct?"

"She deserved that and more," Miss Upshaw answered.

"Did you ever consider the possibility that Emily heard Harriet scream and, like you, ran into the classroom to see what had happened?" Mr. Crawford asked.

"That is *not* what occurred," Miss Upshaw insisted. "Emily threw that dead bird at Harriet."

"I asked only if you *considered* any other possibilities before you struck Emily," Mr. Crawford repeated.

"There was no need to," Miss Upshaw said. "Emily has been a constant cause of trouble in the school. I didn't have to consider alternative possibilities."

"So without bothering to find out any facts, upon seeing Harriet crying and Emily laughing, you struck Emily, then began shaking her, and then struck her again, giving her a black eye," Mr. Crawford said.

"She attacked me," Miss Upshaw retorted. "Mayor Dale, I refuse to put up with any more of this vicious interrogation. *I'm* not on trial here."

"You certainly are not," Mayor Dale assured her, and looked directly at Mr. Crawford. "That will be all, Mr. Crawford. Miss Upshaw, thank you for protecting my daughter, and for all you have done to maintain order in our school in spite of the presence of the Austen girls. Might we hear next from Miss Browne, Judge Cosgrove? She can shed more light on Emily Hasbrouck's pattern of misbehavior."

"Miss Browne, would you come here, please?" Judge Cosgrove said.

Miss Browne took the chair Miss Upshaw had been sitting in.

"I have just a few questions for you, Miss Browne," Mayor Dale said. "But before I begin, I want to commend you on the excellent work you do with the unfortunate girls you must shelter. I know it cannot be an easy job, and I know you want what is best for them."

"Yes, sir, I do," Miss Browne said.

"I just want a little bit of background on Emily Hasbrouck," Mayor Dale said. "Is it safe to say that she was a troublemaker at Austen?"

"Not at the Home itself," Miss Browne corrected him.

"But you did have to punish her, did you not?" Mayor Dale persisted. "Because of her activities at school?"

"Yes, sir," Miss Browne said.

"And she ran away," Mayor Dale said. "And upon her return, you forbade her to live at Austen."

"Yes, I did," Miss Browne admitted.

"So, in fact, Emily Hasbrouck has been expelled once already," Mayor Dale said. "Now, the trouble she got into, was it caused by her attacking my daughter and my daughter's friends?"

"Yes, sir," Miss Browne confirmed.

"And have you ever believed her to be remorseful over her behavior?" Mayor Dale asked.

"Emily felt real grief when Gracie Dodge died," Miss Browne said.

"Gracie was Emily's accomplice," Mayor Dale said. "She too attacked Harriet, Isabella, and in particular poor little Florrie Sheldon. And then after one such vicious attack, while trying to run away, the Gracie girl tripped and hit her head against a rock and died."

"That's not what happened!" Emily shouted.

"Mr. Crawford, will you please advise the girl to keep quiet?" Judge Cosgrove said. "She does her cause no good by such antics."

"Miss Browne, you were telling us about Gracie," Mayor Dale continued. "And how her unfortunate death was a result of her own cruelty, led on by Emily Hasbrouck."

"That is the story as I was told it," Miss Browne said.

"A story, you say," Mr. Keller said. "Does that mean you believe it happened some other way?"

"I wasn't there," Miss Browne said. "Emily said the incident happened one way. Harriet, Isabella, and Florrie said it happened a different way."

"And whose word are you more likely to believe?" Mr. Sheldon asked. "A stray taken in out of charity, or three girls from the best families in this town?"

"I didn't accept Emily's version," Miss Browne replied. "And when Judge Cosgrove called me and said not to allow Emily back, I went along with it. But

Emily isn't all bad. Far from it. If you could just find it in your hearts not to expel her, I'm sure something could be worked out."

"Thank you, Miss Browne," Mayor Dale said brusquely. "I think we've heard enough from both Miss Upshaw and Miss Browne to render our decision. They both have declared that Emily Hasbrouck has been a troublemaker since her arrival in Oakbridge. She was allowed to live here in spite of the fact there was a poorhouse in the town she was brought up in. But because of misbegotten charity, she has tormented Isabella Cosgrove, poor little Florrie Sheldon, and my own daughter, Harriet. Worse still, she has influenced other Austen girls to do the same. She is thus responsible for the death of one of those girls, and it is simply good fortune that has kept her from doing more serious bodily harm to the good children of this town—"

"If you please, just wait a second," Mr. Crawford interrupted. "Aren't you going to allow Emily to speak in her own defense?"

"That isn't necessary," Judge Cosgrove replied. "The facts have been laid out in a quite convincing manner."

"But what if I can prove that Emily didn't bring the dead bird into school?" Mr. Crawford asked.

"That's irrelevant," Judge Cosgrove said. "No matter who brought it in, Emily threw it at Harriet Dale. I'm quite satisfied we know who the culprit is and what the appropriate punishment should be."

"No! No! You do not, sir!"

Emily turned at the sound of a woman's voice from the back of the room.

"You must let me speak before you vote," the woman said. "I insist upon it."

"And who might you be, madam?" Judge Cosgrove asked.

The woman walked to the front of the room. "My name is Mrs. John Winston," she said. "It was my son Johnny who left that dead bird in Emily Hasbrouck's desk."

"That may well be, madam," Judge Cosgrove said. "But I have just declared that irrelevant to these proceedings."

"I'm sorry, sir, but it is relevant," Mrs. Winston said. "My boy Johnny is nine years old. And he's a good boy. He's never gotten into trouble before. But last night he admitted to us that he left a threatening note in Emily's desk, and then the bird, and worse still, he threw a rock into the Webbers' front parlor. The rock struck Bessie Webber, and it's a miracle she wasn't more badly hurt."

"You need to punish your son, but I still fail to see the relevance in all this," Mayor Dale said. "We had agreed to vote."

"I will not be quiet," Mrs. Winston insisted. "I've been quiet too long. Johnny did all those cruel things because he was desperate for Emily to leave Oakbridge. Not that he knew the girl. He didn't. But he'd heard his father and me having terrible arguments about her, and he thought the only way he could stop those arguments would be if Emily left town."

"What caused those arguments?" Mr. Thompkins asked.

"This is a terrible thing for me to admit," Mrs. Winston said. "My husband has begged me not to. He works for Mr. Sheldon at the mill. He's head bookkeeper there, and he is convinced if I tell the truth he'll lose his job. But my silence is hurting too many innocent people, and even worse, it's turning my son into a vicious attacker. For his sake, I must tell the truth."

"And what is that truth?" Reverend Jones asked.

"A few weeks ago, I was in my front parlor," Mrs. Winston said. "I was looking out on the street, waiting for Johnny to return from playing. I saw two of the Austen girls there, which surprised me since they usually go back to the home directly from school. And I saw three other girls with them. I knew those girls to be Harriet Dale, Isabella Cosgrove, and Florrie Sheldon. It was a warm day, and I had my window open. I could hear some of what was being said. Harriet used a word to describe the girls—well, it's a word I would not use. It was clear to me that Harriet, Isabella, and Florrie were insulting the two Austen girls. Isabella even threatened to have them sent to jail if they continued to walk on the sidewalk."

"That's just what happened," Emily whispered. "Someone saw what happened!"

"Of course I didn't know the Austen girls," Mrs. Winston said. "I've always told my children not to associate with them at school. But they were easy to identify, because of their uniforms. One of them had long hair, and the other very short-cropped hair. Harriet Dale pushed the short-haired girl onto the street. The long-haired girl refused to join her there. Florrie Sheldon screamed for the other girls to push her onto the street, and they did. Harriet Dale and Isabella Cosgrove pushed her with all their might into the middle of the street. The girl fell and never got up again. When they saw that she was seriously hurt, Harriet and Isabella ran off. Florrie couldn't because of her leg. I telephoned Dr. Edwards, but by the time I got through, he had already been summoned. I could hear him say the long-haired girl was dead."

The entire room burst into talk. Aunt Bessie and Miss Alice both hugged Emily.

"I told my husband what I had seen," Mrs. Winston continued. "And he told me to keep it to myself because of Florrie Sheldon's involvement. I convinced myself it was none of my business. I even said to myself that the girl who had died had no family, no one who cared about her, as if that somehow made her death less important. And then the short-haired girl—I learned her name was Emily Hasbrouck—well, she left school for a few days, and I thought no one would know what the truth was. But when she returned I began to worry, and my husband and I began to quarrel. And it was those quarrels that my son heard, and he thought if he could only chase Emily out of town, the truth would never be known and his father wouldn't lose his job."

Mrs. Winston paused for a moment and looked straight at Emily. "I'm sorry," she said. "Sorrier than you will ever know. I've always believed the Austen girls weren't as good as we were. When I went to school I was cruel to the Austen girls in my class, just as all my friends were. But now I see what that thoughtless cruelty can lead to. A girl is dead because of it, and our children, my son among them, have become violent, even to the point of killing. This must stop before our own cruelty destroys us. I am so terribly sorry."

Mr. Crawford stood up. "Is there any reason now to continue this hearing?" he asked. "Surely you understand why Emily behaved the way she did. She has been provoked and terrorized by the so-called good children of this town. It is she who is owed the apologies."

"N-Nonsense," Mayor Dale sputtered. "It's all lies. I vote for the expulsion of Emily Hasbrouck before more such slanders are spoken."

"I agree," Mr. Sheldon said. "Mrs. Winston, your husband was quite right to worry about his employment. I vote for Emily Hasbrouck's expulsion as well."

"I vote against it," Reverend Jones said.

"I vote against it also," Mr. Schmidt said.

"It's a horror what's been done to that child," Mr.

Thompkins said. "I vote against the expulsion, and I seriously suggest we investigate Miss Upshaw's conduct with the Austen girls."

That was three votes for Emily and two against. All Mr. Keller had to do was vote for Emily and it would prove that her story was the true one. Emily couldn't believe it. Not only would she not be expelled, but the truth about Gracie had come out.

"With a heavy heart, I vote for expulsion," Mr. Keller said. "In spite of what Mrs. Winston believes she saw, Emily Hasbrouck is clearly a wicked troublemaker, and we will all be better off without her."

Emily gasped. How could he do that? Now Judge Cosgrove was sure to vote for expulsion, and it wouldn't matter what the truth was.

Judge Cosgrove sat at the center of the table. The room had turned deathly silent. "I had hoped not to have to vote," he said. "The president votes only when there is a tie, and I had hoped there would be no such tie."

What was he waiting for? Emily knew, they all knew, what his vote was going to be.

Judge Cosgrove closed his eyes. Emily thought she could see a tear emerge from one of them. "My daughter Isabella has not been well," he said. "Last night, after she heard about the rock hitting Bessie Webber, she became truly hysterical. My wife and I sat with her for many hours, until she finally told us what was disturbing her. It seems she feels haunted by Gracie

Dodge's death. Because she and Harriet pushed Gracie onto that street.

"I never wanted it to come out," the judge continued. "I would do anything to protect my child. We all would. I told myself if the vote went in favor of expulsion, as I was sure it would, no harm would be done. Emily Hasbrouck would be better off outside Oakbridge. If need be, I would anonymously try to find a placement for her elsewhere. I have relatives out West who could use a young servant girl. She wouldn't starve or end up in the poorhouse. I knew I owed her that much, since it was I who insisted she not be allowed back to the Austen Home.

"But the vote is tied, and I must vote against expulsion. I have sinned against Emily Hasbrouck. We all have. I can only hope God will one day forgive us."

"That's it," Mr. Crawford said. "We've won, Emily!"

But Emily was too shocked to celebrate. And she couldn't be sure just what the nature of her victory was.

Eleven

It hadn't taken much begging on Emily's part to be excused from school on Friday. She spent a quiet weekend with the Webbers, the only real distraction being a formal apology from Johnny Winston. Miss Alice and Miss Browne had several telephone conversations, which Emily knew concerned her, but she refused to think about them. Her future was no more in her own hands than it ever had been. But at least she'd accomplished what she'd returned to Oakbridge to do. The truth had been revealed about Gracie's death.

Emily found on Mondy morning that she was as nervous about returning to school as she had been the day she first came back. But this time Aunt Bessie didn't accompany her. She was still recovering from the blow to her head. And Miss Alice walked her only to the schoolyard. "You'll be fine from here," she said, patting Emily's arm.

Emily had her doubts, but she said nothing. It helped

when Constance joined her and they walked in together.

The first thing Emily saw was that her desk was no longer in the hallway. She went into the classroom to get it and found someone other than Mrs. Hearst standing by the door.

"Are you Emily Hasbrouck?" the woman asked.

"Yes, ma'am," Emily answered.

"I'm Mrs. Follett. I'm going to be teaching this class from now on," the woman explained.

Oh, no, Emily thought. Mrs. Hearst has been fired after all.

"You've been asked to go to the principal's office immediately," Mrs. Follett said.

"Why?" Constance asked. "Emily didn't do anything wrong."

"I don't know why," Mrs. Follett said. "I was simply requested to convey that message. Emily, I trust you know where the office is."

"Yes, ma'am," Emily said. "It'll be all right, Constance." She only wished she could believe it. But Miss Upshaw had obviously figured out yet another form of punishment for her, and deserved or not, Emily would have to endure it.

When she entered the principal's office, it wasn't Miss Upshaw she saw, but Mrs. Hearst. And standing by Mrs. Hearst's side was Harriet Dale.

"Hello, Emily," Mrs. Hearst said.

"Miss Upshaw told me to come," Emily said.

Mrs. Hearst laughed. "It was I who requested it," she said. "Because of ill health, Miss Upshaw has been asked to leave her position here. I'm the acting principal."

"You are?" Emily said. "I mean, that's wonderful."

"Thank you," Mrs. Hearst said. "I shall try to do my best. I thought a good place to start would be with apologies from Harriet, Isabella, and Florrie. But Isabella and her mother have left town for a few days. And Florrie has been sent to live with her aunt for the remainder of the year. That leaves only Harriet."

Emily stared at Harriet. She looked much smaller, standing all alone, than she had looked with Isabella and Florrie beside her.

"I don't see why I have to apologize," Harriet complained. "She's the one who threw the dead bird at me. I didn't do anything. She should apologize to me."

"I'm sorry," Emily said automatically. "I shouldn't have thrown that bird at you."

"Very well," Mrs. Hearst said. "That apology is out of the way. Now, Harriet, you may commence with yours."

"But I just said I have nothing to apologize for," Harriet said. "And you can't make me say I'm sorry to a girl like that. I'm the mayor's daughter and I don't have to."

"Now let me explain a few things to *you*," Mrs. Hearst said. "There is no such thing as 'a girl like that.' No matter what the past policy has been, from now on every child in this school will be treated equally. Do you understand, Harriet?"

"I understand," Harriet muttered.

"Very well," Mrs. Hearst said. "Now, it is true you had nothing to do with the dead bird, and I know you were upset when Emily threw it at you—an act for which she just apologized. But you have been provoking her and physically attacking her since the day she began school here. For that you owe Emily an apology."

"You can't make me," Harriet said.

Mrs. Hearst picked up the telephone. "Please connect me to the Dale residence," she said.

"No!" Harriet said. "Don't bother Mama."

"I must," Mrs. Hearst said. "Because you're going to be suspended from this school until you apologize to Emily Hasbrouck."

"I'm sorry," Harriet said hastily.

"Please cancel my call," Mrs. Hearst said, and hung up the phone. "That was a good start, Harriet. Now tell Emily just what you're sorry for."

"What do you mean?" Harriet asked. "I said I was sorry. I apologized to her. Now you can't suspend me."

"I can still suspend you," Mrs. Hearst said. "Think, Harriet. What could you have done to Emily that would warrant an apology?"

Harriet stood so still, Emily could see she was actually trying to think. Emily tried hard not to smile at the sight.

"I don't know," Harriet said. "I'm just sorry. That's all."

"Emily, are you satisfied with that?" Mrs. Hearst asked.

Part of Emily wanted to say yes. Even a simple, dishonest apology from Harriet was far more than she'd ever anticipated hearing. But then she thought about Gracie and about Mary Kate and decided it wasn't enough.

"No," she said. "I want Harriet to apologize for pushing Gracie into the street. And for calling her a mean name. And for making me walk in the street. And for kicking me. And for lying about me. And for being cruel to the other Austen girls. And for threatening Miss Alice."

Harriet looked sullen. "I'm sorry," she said.

"No," Emily said. "You have to apologize for all those things. You can't just say you're sorry. Start with Gracie. You killed Gracie. You pushed her and she died. Start by saying how sorry you are that you killed her. Start there, Harriet."

Harriet looked dumbstruck. "I didn't make her die! I didn't mean for that to happen," she said. "I was just having some fun. She wasn't supposed to get hurt."

"Pushing people may be fun for you," Mrs. Hearst said. "But it isn't fun for the person who gets pushed. Think, Harriet. Think how it would feel if someone pushed you onto the street just to have some fun."

"It was an accident," Harriet insisted.

"No, it wasn't." Emily corrected her. "You and Isabella pushed her. That was no accident."

"It wasn't my fault she died," Harriet repeated. "Honest. She just fell the wrong way."

"But she *wouldn't* have fallen at all if *you* hadn't pushed her," Emily accused. "Don't you see that? Don't you see that *you* killed her?"

"No," Harriet retorted. "I didn't mean for it to happen. And it isn't fair. Austen girls have always been treated different. They should be. You can't just change the rules now and expect me to apologize."

"Yes, we can," Mrs. Hearst said. "The rules *are* changed, Harriet. And if you can't understand that what you did was wrong, and that at the very least you owe Emily an apology for all the pain you've caused her, then I must say I worry about you and about the kind of life you're going to lead. Because if you have no conscience at all, Harriet Dale, then you have no chance at a decent life. And it won't help you one bit that your father is the mayor. You'll be condemned to a life without love. Because the wicked are never truly loved, Harriet. They are always alone and they are never happy. Is that what you want for yourself?"

"You don't want to live like that," Emily added. "Believe me. I've been alone for so long now and nobody's loved me. It's not my fault my parents are dead and I have no one to love me. It's awful."

"I'll never be alone like that," Harriet said. "I'm not some stupid orphan."

"I'm not stupid." Emily defended herself. "*You're* the stupid one. You're so stupid you don't even know that what you did was bad. You're so stupid you don't even realize how hard I'm trying to be decent to you. You're so stupid you make me sick. I'm sorry, Mrs. Hearst. I don't want to stay here any longer. May I leave now? Harriet Dale is the most pathetic girl I have ever met."

"Yes, Emily, you may leave," Mrs. Hearst said. "Harriet, I'm going to have to suspend you. I apologize for wasting your time, Emily."

Emily nodded and left the principal's office. She couldn't feel the least bit sorry for Harriet—or, for that matter, for Isabella and Florrie. She just couldn't. They had been cruel and they were finally being punished. They didn't deserve pity.

When she returned to the classroom, she found pandemonium. "Welcome back," Mrs. Follett said. "Harriet isn't with you?"

"She's being suspended," Emily declared, and enjoyed hearing the gasp from the other students.

"All right, then, we'll proceed without her," Mrs. Follett said. "Emily, you look fairly short. We're reorganizing the seating arrangements. From now on shorter children will be in the front, taller ones in the back. I'm trying to line everyone up in size order. Emily, I think you fit in right around here. Yes, that will do. Now, children, one by one, walk to the desks. We'll start with you first, Mary, since you're the shortest."

Emily watched with shock as one of the Austen girls

sat in what had been Harriet's seat. By the time the children had all been given their new seat assignments, the Austen girls were scattered throughout the room. Emily herself was in the second row, with Constance only three chairs away.

One of the other children raised her hand. "You didn't save seats for Harriet or Isabella or Florrie," she said.

"My understanding is that Florrie won't be returning to this school," Mrs. Follett said. "And Isabella's future here is uncertain. Harriet, after her suspension, can take a seat in the back row. She's a tall girl. Now, class, take out your arithmetic books. It's time we got to work."

Emily could hardly concentrate on her schoolwork. She was relieved when Mrs. Follett didn't call on her all morning. By the time the bell rang for lunch, she felt ready to explode.

She followed Constance to the lunchroom. She had always sat with the Austen girls, or in the hallway. It felt strange to take a seat with the other children.

But before she had a chance to take out the sandwich she'd packed that morning, one of the Austen girls walked up to her. Her name was Jane Smith, Emily remembered. She was a year or two older and had been in the dormitory with Emily.

"The other girls asked me to speak to you," Jane explained.

Emily nodded.

"Miss Browne had an assembly for all of us yesterday," Jane said. "To tell us about the changes that were coming. Not sitting in the back anymore. And soon they're going to have us sit with our classes at lunch."

"That'll be nice," Emily answered.

"It'll be different," Jane said. "It's kind of scary. I've lived at Austen all my life. From first grade on, I've sat with the other Austen girls in the back of the lunchroom. I'm not sure I'm going to like sitting with my class. It feels strange enough sitting in the third row, sitting between two children who aren't from Austen. The teacher can see me better now. I won't get away with as much. They never cared before what we did, just as long as we kept quiet. They never called on us. Today my teacher called on me three times just because I wasn't in the back row."

"I'm sorry," Emily said.

"Well, I don't know how much of that is your fault," Jane said. "But we wanted you to know one good thing is going to happen. Well, bad and good. The bad part is Mr. Sheldon isn't going to donate material for our uniforms anymore."

"Oh, no," Emily said. "You're going to wear poorbox clothes?"

Jane grinned. "No, that's the good part," she said. "Judge Cosgrove donated a whole lot of money to buy all kinds of material. And some of the town ladies are going to come to the Home and we're all going to sew up new dresses together. It was this woman named Mrs.

Winston's idea. Dresses and skirts and blouses. All different colors. Can you believe it?"

"That's wonderful," Emily said. "Judge Cosgrove is actually doing that?"

Jane nodded. "He was there," she said. "At the assembly. He said we were part of the community and it was about time we were treated that way. And for supper that night, we had cake. It was like Christmas. You should have seen Miss Browne. She just kept smiling. And Judge Cosgrove also said he was going to start a committee to raise money for a scholarship. The Gracie Dodge Scholarship, he called it, for an outstanding girl from Austen to go to college. Can you imagine? No girl from Austen has ever gone to college."

"That's wonderful," Emily said.

"Anyway, we wanted you to know," Jane said. "Before, nobody cared about us. The only time they noticed us was when something bad happened. Of course now we're going to have to pay attention in school, things like that." She was quiet for a moment. "It's too late for me," she said. "I'll just leave school at the end of eighth grade, the way I always planned to. But for the younger girls, now, maybe they have a chance. They're the only family I have, and I'm glad for them. So I thought you should know."

"Thank you," Emily said. "And tell them how happy I am for them."

"I will," Jane said, and she walked back to the other Austen girls.

"Gee, it sounds great," Constance said. "Maybe you should move back."

Emily remembered the pervasive loneliness at Austen. "No, thank you," she said.

"Are you still going to have to live with your uncle?" Constance asked.

"I guess so," Emily said. "I haven't heard otherwise."

"We're going to be moving soon too," Constance said. "To Boston, I think. The union wants Father there."

"Boston is so far away," Emily said.

"I'm used to moving," Constance said. "Besides, you're my only friend here, and you'll be gone too."

"We're always going to be friends," Emily said. "We'll write long letters to each other."

"I'd like that," Constance said. "I've never gotten letters before."

"I got one once," Emily said. "And it made me feel better to hear from her. I'll like getting letters from you. It'll make it easier for me when I have to live with the Hasbroucks."

"I'll miss you," Constance said.

"I'll miss you too," Emily said. And for the first time she realized she was going to miss Oakbridge as well.

Twelve

"My," Aunt Bessie said on Saturday. "I can't get over how much you resemble Emily."

Emily looked at the man who was her uncle. He reminded her strongly of her father. No wonder Aunt Mabel looked at Emily and saw Hasbrouck. She looked like one.

"It's very kind of you to invite me here," Mr. Hasbrouck said. "And your generosity in tending to my niece all these weeks. Well, I can never express how grateful I am."

"We love Emily," Miss Alice said. "She's a wonderful girl. She'll always be a part of our family. In fact, I'm planning on asking her to be one of my bridesmaids."

"You are?" Emily asked.

"Would you like that?" Miss Alice asked.

"Oh, yes," Emily said. "More than anything."

"Emily is lucky to have such good friends," Mr. Hasbrouck said.

"And we're lucky to have her," Aunt Bessie replied.

"Mother, why don't we prepare some tea for our guest?" Miss Alice said. "That will give Emily and her uncle a chance to talk."

"Very well," Aunt Bessie said. "Emily, if you should need us, we'll just be in the kitchen."

"Mother," Miss Alice said, but Emily was grateful for Aunt Bessie's reassurances.

"I do see your father's face in you," Mr. Hasbrouck said. "Did he ever speak of me?"

Emily shook her head. They were sitting in the parlor. The window had been repaired, but it still made Emily nervous to remember what had happened. Not that she needed anything more to affect her nerves. Being alone with a Hasbrouck was enough.

"There were six in our family," Mr. Hasbrouck began. "Four boys, two girls. Your father was the youngest, I was second from the oldest. There was five years between us in age, and I left home at fifteen. So I didn't know your father all that well. But he was my brother and I should have made an effort to learn what had become of him."

"He died three years ago," Emily said.

Mr. Hasbrouck nodded. "So Miss Browne told me," he said. "Do you know much about your Hasbrouck relatives? I know you were brought up by your mother's aunt, Mabel Lathrop."

"She didn't much care for Hasbroucks," Emily said.

"Neither did I," Mr. Hasbrouck said. "My father was a cruel and deceitful man. My mother loved us as best she could, but with so many young children it was more than she could handle. She died when I was twelve and your father seven. My older brother, Teddy, was already a thief. His arrest, I think, was what broke my mother's heart and led to her premature death. It was on her grave that I vowed never to follow in my father's footsteps. I wouldn't drink, I wouldn't steal, and I wouldn't hurt others."

"My father didn't steal," Emily said. "And he never hurt me. Except sometimes when he was drunk, and then he was always sorry after."

"That's how it is with drink," Mr. Hasbrouck said. "My father never cared who he beat when he was drunk, but afterwards he always felt remorse toward my mother and sisters. He taught us boys never to strike a woman, but we saw him strike them repeatedly under the influence of alcohol."

"And you don't drink at all?" Emily asked. Her uncle seemed a most unlikely Hasbrouck.

"On my eighteenth birthday I broke my vow," Mr. Hasbrouck confided. "I had run away from home three years earlier. For three years I had taken any kind of work I could find. I associated with the roughest sorts of men and had temptations thrust at me all the time. But I remembered my mother, and the life she had been forced to lead, and I resisted those temptations. Only I weakened on my eighteenth birthday."

"And what happened?" Emily asked.

Mr. Hasbrouck laughed. "Nothing much, really," he

said. "I woke up the next morning with a terrible head-ache, but that was about it for physical damage. But inside I felt sick at having given in. I knew the dangers of drink. I thought about my father and I realized I could not imagine what he would be like sober. I went back home then, to see if he had changed, and found he had not, and yet another of my brothers was in jail, and one of my sisters had already been lost to the streets. Your father and my youngest sister were all that remained in the household. I sat them down and told them they didn't have to be like their father. They could lead clean lives and marry decent people. My baby sister laughed at me. I'll never forget the sound of that laugh. But I think your father understood me."

"He loved my mother," Emily said. "I know he did. She died when my sister was born and he never got over it."

"I should have taken him with me when I left," Mr. Hasbrouck said. "But I didn't know what was going to become of me, and I had no idea how I could care for a thirteen-year-old boy. I was sure the only way I could lead a decent life was to act as though my family were dead. For the second time, I stood at my mother's grave and made my vows. But this time I vowed to have nothing to do with my family again. I left my hometown and spent years wandering around, working wherever I could. It was a hard life, but it was an honest one, and it was the only kind I was used to."

Emily looked at her uncle. He was dressed in a suit

and had a gold pocket watch. She didn't have much experience with men, but he looked more like a lawyer than a laborer.

Her uncle smiled. "When I was twenty, I was hit by a runaway horse and buggy," he said. "It was clear my injuries weren't too serious. The town where it happened had no doctor. I was taken to the town's pharmacist. He took care of all the minor injuries and illnesses. His name was James Hamilton, and he was as good a man as I've ever met. He tended to my wounds, and we began to talk. He heard my story, and something in it touched his heart. He took me home to meet his family. That was the luckiest day of my life, for his daughter was there. Betsy was just seventeen and I swear she won my heart the moment I first saw her."

"Did you marry her?" Emily asked.

"That I did," her uncle replied, smiling. "Thanks to Mr. Hamilton I trained as an apothecary and he took me into his business and let me take over. Betsy and I have been married for twenty years now. We have a son, Jimmy, and a daughter, Dorothy. Jimmy has just started college, and it's his dream to be a doctor someday. Dorothy is fifteen and some days she wants to be a nurse, other days a teacher. And then there are days she wants to marry and raise a dozen children. When the time comes, I'm sure she'll make the right choice."

Emily didn't know what to make of all this. A Hasbrouck as respectable as any Lathrop. Aunt Mabel would be more than surprised.

Mr. Hasbrouck looked at her. "I've been doing all the talking," he said. "Betsy sometimes complains I won't let her get a word in edgewise. Tell me a bit about yourself, Emily."

"I like to play the piano," Emily said.

"Do you really?" Mr. Hasbrouck said. "We have a piano in our home. Betsy loves to play, and both Jimmy and Dorothy have had lessons. Even I try to pick out a tune now and then." He laughed, and Emily found it was a nice kind of laugh. "See, I'm doing it again," he said. "You say five words and I counter with a hundred. Tell me some more, and I'll try to keep quiet."

"I don't know," Emily continued, trying to figure out what to say about herself. "I lived with my aunt Mabel and she taught me how to do all kinds of housework. I'm really very useful. I can sew and clean and cook. I did all that for her last year. She didn't even need to keep a servant, I was so good at it. I'm in sixth grade and I'm good at my classes. And I'm a good girl. Really I am. I was in a lot of trouble here, but it wasn't my fault. Aunt Bessie and Miss Alice have been wonderful to take me in. Aunt Mabel was a true Christian to let me live with her. She kept me on the path of righteousness. I lived for a little while at the Austen Home for Orphaned Girls. I had two friends there, Mary Kate and Gracie. Only Gracie died and Mary Kate ran away. But I have another friend now, Constance Crawford. I go to Oakbridge Primary School, because the school board voted not to expel me. But I'm not happy there.

You'd think I would be, because everybody knows now what Harriet and Isabella and Florrie did. Things are much better. I get to sit in the classroom now with everyone else. But Constance is still my only friend and her family is going to move soon. And then I'll be alone again."

"Miss Webber and Miss Browne have both told me of your troubles," Mr. Hasbrouck said. "I think you must be very brave."

"I'm not," Emily said, shaking her head. "Gracie was brave. I wish I was more like her."

"I didn't think I was brave either," Mr. Hasbrouck said. "Until Jim Hamilton proved to me I was. That's one of my many debts to him. I gather you feel indebted too."

"Yes, sir," Emily said. "To Aunt Mabel and to Miss Browne and to Aunt Bessie and Miss Alice."

Mr. Hasbrouck nodded. "I think it's different for people like us," he said. "I know I had a father, and a slew of brothers and sisters, but still I'd fended for myself since I was not that much older than you. Any act of kindness shown to me, well, I just felt like a dog thrown a bone. Do you know that feeling?"

"Oh, yes, sir, I do," Emily said. "Aunt Bessie and Miss Alice actually get mad at me sometimes because I thank them too much."

"That's because they don't know what it's like to have no one," he said. "They're used to love, so it's easy for them to give and to receive. But for me at least, and

I suspect for you, love's kind of a miracle. It's as if we don't deserve it. My wife and children, they take love for granted. But I don't seem to be able to. I suspect you don't take much for granted either, do you, Emily?"

"No, sir," Emily said. "Nothing good anyway."

"My father-in-law lived with us until the day he died," Mr. Hasbrouck explained. "That was almost two years ago. His room's been empty ever since. Betsy and Dorothy have been champing at the bit for the past two weeks, ever since we learned about you. Dorothy has all kinds of ideas on how to turn it into a pretty bedroom for a girl your age."

"You don't have to do that for me," Emily said. "I can sleep someplace else if it's more convenient."

"If you come to live with me, you'll be part of my family," Mr. Hasbrouck said. "We won't be hiding you away in the attic. We won't be treating you like a guest either. Jimmy helps with the outdoor chores, and Dorothy sets the table and does mending with her mother. I don't know what Betsy will find for you to do, but I'm sure there'll be something."

"I'm not afraid of work," Emily said.

"I never thought you were," Mr. Hasbrouck said. "You'll have chores to do the same as my other children. We'll be at you to do your schoolwork. There's nothing more important in life than education. I came to mine late, so I appreciate it all the more. But there'll be time for playing the piano and having friends and thinking about boys. Dorothy thinks about boys a lot, so I suspect you will soon enough."

Emily blushed.

"Now I'm doing all the talking again," Mr. Hasbrouck said. "Tell me, Emily, what do you want?"

Emily was startled by the question. "What I want doesn't matter," she said.

"It matters to me," he said.

Emily stared at the man. He looked like her father, he even sounded a little bit like him. And she could tell that he wasn't just respectable, he was kind. And he understood her. Emily didn't think anybody had ever really understood her before, had known what it felt like to be grateful for bones.

"Do you really want to know what I want?" she asked.

Her uncle nodded.

"I'd like to stay here just a little while longer and visit with you and your family first," Emily said. "Ever since Aunt Mabel died, I've been dreaming about a real home and a real family. I thought my sister's family would want me but they didn't. Then Miss Alice took me in, and I thought they'd let me stay forever, but they can't. Miss Alice will be marrying in a few months, and that's going to change everything. I even dreamed Constance's family would take me in. Constance doesn't even like her bedroom. Am I making any sense?"

"Oh, yes," her uncle said. "I know just what you mean. Many was the time I had those same feelings."

"So now you're saying you'll take me in and give me my own room and let me play the piano and go to school and do all the things I've dreamed of," Emily said. "And my heart is saying 'Oh, yes, oh, yes,' but my head is thinking about all those dreams I've had and how none of them worked out. Maybe your wife will hate me. Maybe Dorothy won't like me because I don't think about boys all the time. Maybe it'll bother you to have another Hasbrouck living with you. And then I'll be on my own again with no one to turn to and I just couldn't bear it. Not again. Not so soon."

"I know that won't happen," Mr. Hasbrouck said. "But I don't blame you for worrying about it. Do you think if you visited over Thanksgiving, and got to meet your aunt and your cousins, it would help?"

"Yes, sir," Emily said. "I'm sorry if I don't seem grateful. I am, I really am. If you've changed your mind, I'll certainly understand. Or if you think now I don't deserve to be treated like one of your family, but you're willing to take me on as a servant, then that's all right too. At least that way I wouldn't be worrying all the time that I was doing something wrong. I know how to work. I just don't know how to be part of a family."

"I had to learn how myself," Mr. Hasbrouck admitted. "In some ways I'm still learning. You have a sister you don't know. My brother was a stranger to me. But I've come back for you, to make you a part of my family. If you want to visit first, and it's all right with the Webbers, I certainly understand."

"It will be," Emily said. "Aunt Bessie told me I could stay here until I was sure about what I wanted to do. Besides, she was worried you might be a white slaver. But I guess you're not that."

Mr. Hasbrouck laughed. "That I'm not," he said. "I'm a happy uncle who's brought you a present. It's nothing much, really. Actually, it was Betsy's idea. We wanted to get you something, and we didn't know what you looked like or what you liked to do. Betsy said she was sure you'd like this." Mr. Hasbrouck handed a bag over to Emily. "Dorothy suggested that we should wrap it in some pretty paper, but it was such a funny shape, we thought we'd just let you have it in this. I hope you like it."

Emily opened the bag. In it was a beautiful white bow for her hair. "Oh, Mr. Hasbrouck," she said. "It's so lovely. I've dreamed of something this special for a long time."

"I'm your uncle Nathan, Emily," Mr. Hasbrouck said. "Please call me that."

"Uncle Nathan." Emily said his name in almost a whisper. Then she called out, "Aunt Bessie! Miss Alice! Come into the parlor and see what my uncle Nathan brought me!" As Emily tried with trembling hands to put on the hair bow, she looked at the man who looked like her father, who looked like her, and she knew she was halfway home.

About the Author

Susan Beth Pfeffer is the author of both middle-grade and young adult fiction. Her most recent middle-grade novels include *The Pizza Puzzle* and *Nobody's Daughter*, the companion to *Justice for Emily*. Her highly praised *The Year Without Michael* is an ALA Best Book for Young Adults, an ALA YALSA Best of the Best, and a *Publishers Weekly* Best Book of the Year. Her novels for young adults include *Twice Taken*, *Most Precious Blood*, *About David*, and *Family of Strangers*. Susan Beth Pfeffer lives in Middletown, New York.